The Bachelor

That's Randall Watson, who's learned the hard way there's no such thing as true love. So when he finds out his grandmother's *eloped*, he knows he has to find her and talk some sense into her. And he's taking…

The Beauty

…Gina Leigh, who's about the only person in the world the runaway bride might actually listen to. So even though she actually approves of this "romantic foolishness," she's coming along as he drives through…

The Blizzard

…which is so bad that before long they're stranded in a little town with exactly *one* vacant hotel room left, and staring at…

The Bed

…the very, very small bed that they'll be sharing for what may just be the longest, *hottest* night of their lives.…

Dear Reader,

I don't know where you live; it could be a nice, warm, *snowless* place. Southern California, maybe, or Florida. Or Hawaii. But as for me, I live right in the snow belt: Connecticut. And I grew up in an even worse spot, weatherwise: western New York state. So I know what blizzards are, because I've had to cope with quite a few in my time. In fact, just a few years ago, we got so many snowstorms—and I had to shovel the driveway so many times—that I joked to all my friends about how I was going steady with my snow shovel. I figured he was the strong, silent type, and he got me out of the house on a regular basis. However, given the opportunity, I would have been happy to trade him in for Randall Watson, the hero of Maris Soule's *The Bachelor, the Beauty and the Blizzard.* If you read the book, I think you'll see why.

While you're in a reading mood, be sure to pick up Mary Starleigh's *The Texan and the Pregnant Cowgirl.* This brand-new author is someone to watch, because she not only has talent, she also has a great sense of humor. And on top of that, she knows all about ostriches and somehow manages to make the crazy critters a perfect part of a perfect romance. Check this one out; you won't be disappointed.

And then come back again next month, for two more great books all about meeting—and marrying!—Mr. Right.

Yours,

Leslie Wainger
Senior Editor and Editorial Coordinator

Please address questions and book requests to:
Silhouette Reader Service
U.S.: 3010 Walden Ave., P.O. Box 1325, Buffalo, NY 14269
Canadian: P.O. Box 609, Fort Erie, Ont. L2A 5X3

MARIS SOULE

The Bachelor, the Beauty and the Blizzard

'98

Maris Soule

SILHOUETTE YOURS TRULY™

Published by Silhouette Books

America's Publisher of Contemporary Romance

My thanks to Ann Larkin, who was an inspiration for this book. Her energy, smiles and laughter are an example that life can be enjoyed at any age. I treasure our friendship. And thanks to my aunt and uncle, who helped me with the information about Rossmoor. They, too, are examples of people enjoying the "golden" years.

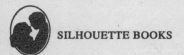 SILHOUETTE BOOKS

ISBN 0-373-52067-0

THE BACHELOR, THE BEAUTY AND THE BLIZZARD

Copyright © 1998 by Maris Soule

Printed in U.S.A.

About the author

I was born and raised in California and fell in love with the Lake Tahoe area the first time my parents took me up there to my great-uncle's "cabin" (which looked like a house to me). The only thing that scared me was the drive up Highway 50, with the steep drop-offs along the way. I'd slink down in the back seat and refuse to look out. When I got older, I overcame that problem and enjoyed the drive and the scenery, but I hated it when I had to put chains on the tires, and I remember one time when it took me an hour to dig out the car after a snowstorm.

When I came up with the idea for *The Bachelor, the Beauty and the Blizzard,* it was easy to picture a situation where two people might get caught by the elements in the Sierra Nevadas and be forced to spend time together. And "Grandma" came from two people I know, one a widow, who wrote a letter to an old high school flame after she heard his wife had died, then married him two years later, and the other a waitress in California, who at seventy-three is going strong, loves life and takes off for Reno whenever she can for a weekend of cards.

As for eloping… Well, my husband and I nearly did thirty years ago. We finally decided on a traditional wedding, but the idea still sounds romantic to me.

Maris Soule

Books by Maris Soule

Silhouette Yours Truly

Heiress Seeking Perfect Husband
The Bachelor, the Beauty and the Blizzard

Silhouette Romance

1

"**S**he's gone."

Gina Leigh looked up from her driver's-side door. She'd known that Randall Watson was at his grandmother's from the white Lexus parked in the driveway. What she hadn't expected was for him to run out the front door and yell across the lawn at her.

Concerned that something might have happened to Ella, Gina quickly finished locking her car, dropped her keys in her purse, then started up the concrete walk. "What do you mean she's gone?"

"Gone off with a man." Randall waved a sheet of white paper, the kind Ella Flemming used to write grocery lists and notes to the gardener. "She says they're eloping. *Eloping*," he repeated, as though the idea were totally incredible.

Gina paused at the base of the porch, and for a moment couldn't stop herself from grinning. *Eloping*. How like Ella. How romantic.

"It's not funny," Randall snapped, his eyes narrowing. "She's run off with some gigolo."

Gina stopped smiling. "Jack Longman is *not* a gigolo, and I can understand why Ella's eloping. She probably figured if she didn't, you'd try to stop her."

"Darn right I would. This is ridiculous." He stepped closer, raw determination in his eyes.

The six-inch rise of the porch added to the nine-inch difference in their heights and gave him too much advantage in Gina's opinion. She moved back a pace, allowing herself more space. Still, she had to look up. "No, it isn't ridiculous. This isn't something that just happened. Your grandmother's been in love with Jack since she was in high school."

"Don't even suggest that!" Randall snapped. "She loved my grandfather."

"Yes, she did. And she loved Jack before she met your grandfather. And now that she's found Jack again, their love's been rekindled. She's been trying to tell you that for the past two months but you won't listen."

"So now you're going to tell me what I should listen to?" he grumbled.

Again he stepped toward her, closing the distance between them. But this time, Gina stood her ground. "Someone needs to tell you."

"Like you told me you'd had experience working with older people?" He shook his head. "I never should have hired you. Here I expected you to look after my grandmother, and what do you do? You get her involved in a romance."

"I did not get her involved in a romance. She got herself involved. And I *have* had experience with older people…with my grandmother." Gina looked him directly in the eyes. Into gorgeous brown eyes that were now sparking with anger. Well, let him be angry. None of this was her fault. "I will not take responsibility for a mature woman's actions. If I've learned anything in the past six months, it is that your grandmother does not need a keeper. A friend and companion, yes. A keeper, no."

"She couldn't see, not until two weeks ago," he said gruffly. "You were supposed to watch over her."

His implication that she hadn't done her job irked Gina. "I was hired as a companion. Monday through Friday, eight-thirty till six, I was here. I never missed a day. Never was late. Up until she had that second operation, I drove your grandmother wherever she wanted to go. Fixed her meals. Helped her with her correspondence. Listened to—"

Randall interrupted. "Goaded her into writing to a man she hadn't seen for fifty years or more."

"I did not *goad* her into anything." And Gina wasn't going to let Ella's grandson—good-looking or not—goad her into a corner. "Your grandmother may be seventy-two years old, but she's not ready to be put on a shelf to shrivel up and die. She's had trouble with her eyes, not her mind. She knows what she wants."

"Does she?" Randall didn't believe that for a second. His grandmother had been devastated by the death of his grandfather. Totally distraught. "Or is she just a lonely old woman who's easy prey for a sweet-talking swindler?"

"Oh, come on. Your grandmother is no dummy." Gina lifted her chin defiantly, her blue-gray eyes set with determination. "And Jack is no swindler. She knows this man. They went to high school together."

"That was a long time ago. People change."

"Well, from what he wrote in his letters and said during their conversations, your grandmother didn't think Jack had changed all that much. She said he sounded like the same Jack she knew in high school."

"You read his letters to her?"

"Up until she had that second operation, yes. That was what you hired me to do."

Again, Randall reminded himself that he never should have hired her. Gina might be twenty-five, but she obviously lacked the maturity his grandmother had needed. He'd thought hiring a companion who had a college degree in communications would be good for his grandmother; that someone who liked to talk would help brighten her days while she was waiting for her surgery. He'd figured being with Gina would give her something else to think about. He hadn't planned on his grandmother thinking of marriage.

"Has this guy ever asked her for money?"

"Jack? No. Why would he? He has his own money. He doesn't need any of hers."

"Just because the guy says he has money doesn't mean he does." A swindler would tell a lonely old woman anything, he thought bitterly . "Next thing you know, the guy's got a problem. He's a little short of cash, and could Grandma possibly loan him a little?" Randall knew exactly how it would go. He'd seen it happen with his mother before her so-called boyfriends milked her of all her savings. Heck, his father had tried it with him.

"One thing I learned a long time ago," he began, "is that my grandmother may be intelligent about some things, but she's a sucker when it comes to a hard-luck story. Look at the huge donation she gave to the Children's Hospital last month. And that's not the only charity that has her on its sucker list."

"Your grandmother said the donation to the Children's Hospital was her usual Christmas gift, one she's given for the past twenty pears. And being generous does not make you a sucker."

Randall could tell that Gina didn't get his point. "You may not know this, but my grandmother nearly got taken by one of those so-called charities two years ago."

"She told me. And she appreciates that you figured out

the organization was a hoax. But we're not talking about the same thing here.''

''No, we're not, are we?'' Bilking an old woman out of some money was one thing. Marrying her was another. ''We shouldn't even be talking. We should be doing something.'' He lifted the note he'd found in the house. ''She left this for you. It says you know what's going on, and that you'll understand what she's doing. So explain to me what she's doing, and where she is.''

''That was for me?'' Gina snatched the paper from his hand, turned away from him and began to read what it said.

Randall stood where he was, not sure what else to do but stare at her profile. As much as she irritated him, she also fascinated him. Her shoulder-length taffy-colored hair was being blown by the breeze, exposing just a bit of her neck, and he remembered the one time he'd accidentally touched her face. He'd turned around to say something to her, and she'd been closer than he'd expected. His hand had brushed right over her cheek.

They'd both been surprised by the contact, and he'd jerked his hand back, but not before feeling the velvety soft texture of her skin. Her neck looked as soft.

Soft skin, hard head, he thought. *Stubborn* was the word his grandfather would have used to describe Gina. Carl Flemming had often called his own wife stubborn. Randall remembered how his grandfather would grumble and complain and make his usual threats about leaving ''that stubborn woman.'' But Carl Flemming usually gave in to Ella. The man had adored his wife and she had adored him.

The idea that she was now running off to marry someone else was ridiculous. Randall had seen his grandmother collapse at his grandfather's funeral, had spent long nights with the sobbing woman in the months that followed. She was vulnerable, and the woman he'd hired to watch over her had failed him.

Not that Gina hadn't performed other parts of her job well. He was aware of all she'd done. Gina Leigh was a five-foot-three dynamo. In the past six months, he'd noticed a big change in his grandmother's attitude toward life. Within a month after he'd hired Gina, his grandmother began relating tidbits of information Gina had told her. Soon she was conveying everything from jokes to new scientific discoveries. Gina had reawakened his grandmother's interest in the world around her.

And Gina wasn't content to merely sit around and talk to his grandmother. She'd taken on everything from cleaning cupboards to rearranging furniture. She'd even polished his grandmother's silverware, a task he'd been assigned as a boy and had always hated.

Yes, Gina Leigh was a hard worker, a talker—and a real cutie. But that still didn't excuse her role in his grandmother's disappearance.

Studying Gina's features, he decided that she wasn't conventionally beautiful. Her mouth was a bit too large, her eyes too wide set and her nose too narrow to fit the image of classic beauty. She fit the girl-next-door stereotype better. Wholesome and healthy.

Cute.

Even her clothing fit that image. Today she was wearing a camel-colored coat that nearly matched her hair, dark brown wool slacks, a light green sweater and brown loafers. Certainly nothing provocative. Nothing to stir any feelings of desire.

So why did just looking at her get him thinking illicit thoughts? Thoughts of kissing and touching and much, much more?

Maybe it was the scent of her *perfume that prompted*

those crazy ideas. A breeze was blowing in his direction, and he was tempted to breathe in deeply. He'd noticed Gina's light, flowery scent several times while visiting his grandmother, had noticed it in fact the day she interviewed for the job. It always had the same enticing effect on him.

Oh yes, hiring her had been a mistake, but she'd been like a breath of fresh air when she'd walked into his office. During the interview, she'd been nervous but not shy. She'd smiled a lot, and he'd liked her animation, the soft yet distinct sound of her voice and the energy that seemed to vibrate through her. He'd felt she was just what his grand-mother needed.

Big mistake.

"This is sweet," Gina said after a moment, then turned slightly so she could look up at him. "Can't you tell she's in love?"

"Love?" he scoffed. "Women. You think any time a man says a few sweet words, it's love."

"You're going to tell me your grandfather wasn't in love with Ella?"

"I know he was, but that was different."

"How?"

"It just was different." Certainly different from how his father had treated his mother. Definitely different from the way any of the boyfriends who came after his dad had treated her. "Tell me, has my grandmother even seen this guy? I mean, recently."

"Recently?" Gina considered the question, then shook her head. "No, but they exchanged pictures, and she said he still had the same cocky look he'd had as a teenager. And they've talked on the phone. Talked a lot, in fact. You even mentioned it last month when you got the phone bill."

He remembered the long-distance calls to Danville. And he remembered his grandmother saying she'd been talking to an old friend. He'd thought she meant a female friend. "So what did they talk about? Write about?"

"From what I overheard, most of their conversations were about family and old friends. And a lot of what they wrote to each other was about things they'd done in the past fifty years or so and things they wished they'd done."

"Did she—or you—ever tell him that my grandmother is a very wealthy woman?"

"No. As I said, I don't think it would matter. Jack's—"

"You're sure you didn't tell him?" Randall interrupted.

"Yes, I'm sure." Gina shook her head exasperatedly, then turned away, starting toward her car.

Her departure surprised him. "Where are you going?"

"Home."

"You can't."

She stopped halfway to her car and looked back at him.

"What's the sense of me staying here? Ella's not here, and you don't trust me. "

"You leave and you're fired."

She laughed and waved the note she held. "I think your grandmother just laid me off. She's found another companion."

"I understand you've applied for the public relations position at Flemming's," Randall said quickly, walking toward her. He would use any means he needed to find his grandmother, including bribery and threats. "Do you want to work at Flemming Corporation or not?"

Her reaction was immediate. "Are you threatening me?"

"I'm saying you can forget the job if you walk away from here without telling me where my grandmother is."

"Then you can keep your job." Gina even had a few ideas of what he could do with the job. "It was Ella who badgered me into sending in my résumé anyway. And you don't need me to tell you where she is," she said. "She's already told you. She's with Jack."

"Yes, but where? Where is he?"

Randall had stopped in front of her. Much too close, Gina decided. She didn't like the fact that she could smell his aftershave and that the edge of his suit jacket was blowing up against her coat. But she wouldn't step back, wouldn't let him intimidate her in any way. "How did you even know she wasn't here this morning? You don't usually come over this early."

Again he made a grumbling sound that said volumes about how he didn't like this situation or being called to task. "She left a message on my voice mail at work. She said she was going to be away for a while, catching up on her past, and if I wanted to know anything, I was to come here and see you this morning."

Gina was beginning to get the picture. Ella did want him to know where she'd gone. She'd planted clues. Well, if that was the way Ella wanted it, Gina would play her part. "My guess is she's gone to Rossmoor."

"Rossmoor?" He looked puzzled.

"The retirement community near Walnut Creek. Jack lives there. He's quite a golfer, I take it. According to him, they have a couple of great courses there."

"Okay." Randall nodded. "Then that's where we go."

"We?" She wasn't sure she'd heard him right.

He'd already turned away and was starting back toward the house. "You go ahead and get into the Lexus. I've got to get my coat and lock up."

"Why should I go with you?" Gina didn't move from where she stood.

He kept walking toward the front door. Not once did he look back. "Because, as she said in that note, you know what's going on."

Gina quickly reread the note Ella had left. She'd known what was going on up until this morning, but she didn't have the slightest idea what was going on now. The moment Randall came out of the house, his overcoat slung over one arm, she spoke up. "I can't help you. I didn't know she was going to do this."

"While we're driving to Rossmoor, you can fill me in on the details of this fifty-year-old-plus romance." He kept walking toward his car.

"I know she told you about Jack." Gina had been there one day when Ella brought up the subject. It had been about a month after the first letter to Jack.

"She's told me very little about him. I'm sure you know a helluva lot more." He held open the passenger's door, waiting for her.

Gina remained where she was, undecided. "You just fired me."

"No, I *threatened* to fire you. And you're wrong about being out of a job. Your job hasn't ended. I need you to talk her out of this foolishness."

His stubbornness amazed her. "And what if I don't want to talk her out of 'this foolishness'? What if I think what she's doing is great?"

"Then your job is to convince *me* that my grandmother's running off with a man she hasn't seen for over fifty years is a good idea."

That, she was willing to do. Acquiescing, Gina walked toward the Lexus. Randall waited until she was comfortably seated, then closed the door and walked around to his side of the car. His overcoat was carefully laid across the back seat, and he took a moment to brush a lock of his wind-blown brown hair into place before he started the car. As he reversed out of Ella's driveway, Gina glanced at her Chevy. It would be safe parked on the street, and even in the event of rain, which seemed likely, her windows were rolled up. From Ella's house, she calculated that it shouldn't be more than a forty-five-minute drive to Walnut Creek. Just enough time, she hoped, to convince Randall that Ella was old enough to make up her own mind, and if she wanted to marry a man she'd known over fifty years ago, then he should be happy for her. At the most, Gina estimated, they should only be gone four or five hours. Less than the normal eight she would have worked for Ella. Accompanying Randall was simply a variation on her workday—nothing more.

She turned slightly in her seat so she could look at him. Most men who'd been named Randall would probably be called Randy. Or maybe Rand. Randall was so formal, but even Ella called him by that name. At least, she did most of the time. Once in a while she would slip and call him Randy. Then she would shake her head and say, ''He doesn't like to be called that.''

She'd explained why once. ''It reminds him of his father. Randy means lustful and lecherous, and if ever there was a randy fellow, it was Randall's father.''

Well, as far as Gina could tell, Randall Watson was not the typical lecherous male, even though she'd seen him in the company of several different women over the past six months. Actually, when describing him to her roommate, the only image Gina could come up with was ''businessman.'' Whenever Randall Watson stopped by the house to visit Ella, the conversation would usually turn to the Flemming Corporation. He seemed to love discussing this quarter's profits and next quarter's projected losses. And with Gina, it was his grandmother he discussed. Had she taken her pills? Put the drops in her eyes? Taken a nap?

In the time she'd known him, Gina couldn't remember Randall cracking a joke, couldn't remember hearing him laugh, and he rarely smiled. Which was probably good because the few glimpses she'd gotten had *done strange* things to her. And *getting weak in the knees at a man's smile* just wasn't like her.

Considering that most of their talks usually ended in arguments, it was really amazing that he hadn't fired her months ago. She knew she was the employee and he was the employer—not to mention Ella's grandson—but she simply couldn't keep her mouth shut when he tried to treat Ella more like a child than a mature woman.

There were a lot of things she knew she shouldn't do as an employee. Mostly she shouldn't be looking at him and having lustful thoughts.

She'd never seen the man wear anything but a suit, usually blue or gray, but occasionally the brown one he had on today. And she'd tried not to think about it, but every so often she'd wondered what he would look like without any clothes on. She had noticed, when he took off his jacket and loosened his tie, that he had a good body. And when he leaned over or reached up, the material of his shirt stretched tight over his back, and it was impossible to miss the lean, rippling play of his muscles. It was also impossible not to do a little lusting.

All in all, it was safer for him to keep his jacket on. Safer to think of him as the enemy. She wanted him to be untouchable, unattainable. then she wouldn't be tempted to touch. Or even have the desire to flirt with him.

Leaning back in the seat, she gazed out the windshield. "Okay, fire away," she said. "What do you want to know about your grandmother and Jack?"

"How in the hell he got her address in the first place."

"She sent it to him."

Randall glanced her way, and Gina remembered back to that morning months ago.

* * *

"I got a call last night," Ella said the moment Gina stepped into the kitchen. "A call from my friend Cora. She'd been to this dinner or meeting or whatever, and ran into an old boyfriend of mine."

"An old boyfriend?" Gina sat down on the chair opposite Ella. The older woman's eyes were blurry with the cataracts that had stolen her vision, but her smile was radiant.

"I haven't heard from Jack in more than fifty years. I knew he was back living in California, but I hadn't tried to contact him. After all, I was married and he was married. I figured too much time had passed." Ella sighed, her shoulders sagging and the smile fading. "Time. It steals so much."

Gina knew that Ella was thinking of the loss of her husband. Although Gina had only seen photos of Carl Flemming, Ella had brought him alive with her stories of how the two had met and all they'd gone through in the forty-five years they were married. Carl Flemming was gone, but Ella hadn't gotten over his passing.

Ella lifted her head, the smile returning. "I almost forgot what I was telling you. Anyway, Cora said that Jack was there, at some Republican Party function. Alone. His wife, it seems, passed on last year. Cancer." Ella shook her head. "Quite an ordeal for him, according to Cora."

"That's a shame," Gina said, not envying anyone who had to watch someone they cared for suffer with cancer.

"My feelings exactly. And I'm sure he's feeling loneliness and a certain amount of guilt because he's alive and she's not. I know how I felt when I lost Carl. So I was thinking of writing to Jack, express my sympathies. It might help him to hear from someone who's also lost a loved one."

"It probably would."

"So will you write a letter for me?" Ella asked. "It would mean a lot to me...and to Jack, I'm sure."

"And that's how it all started?" Randall asked, steering the Lexus onto the interstate.

"Actually, it started way back when your grandmother was in high school," Gina said. "I know she told you that."

He shrugged. "I think she did." He hated to admit that he really hadn't listened to his grandmother all that closely.

"It was her parents who put an end to the romance. They didn't approve of Jack, didn't think he would amount to anything, so they sent your grandmother back East to live with her aunt and go to college there."

"Out of sight, out of mind," Randall muttered, wishing Jack Longman had *stayed* out of sight and out of his grandmother's mind.

Glancing over at Gina, he had a feeling "out of sight and out of mind" might be better where she was concerned. Gina could give him details about this Jack Longman that might be important, but being around her for any extended amount of time wasn't necessarily a good idea. Their encounters always left him feeling off-kilter. He was never sure how to act. Never quite in control.

He looked forward again. It really didn't matter, he acknowledged. Leaving her behind wouldn't have helped. Lately he'd noticed Gina Leigh was never truly out of his mind.

2

The drive to Rossmoor took an hour and it was drizzling by the time they arrived at the gate. All cars entering the area had to pass by a booth manned by a uniformed guard. A simple wave sent the residents on; a sign warned visitors to stop. Randall pulled up beside the booth and lowered his window. "Could you tell me where Jack Longman lives?" he asked the gray-haired guard.

"Is he expecting you?" the guard asked, glancing down at a clipboard.

"No." Randall looked over at Gina, giving her just the hint of a smile, then he looked back at the guard. "Or maybe he is."

She caught his meaning. Randall saw life in terms of prey and predator. In his opinion, Jack was the predator, and Ella was the prey. The predator would be wary.

"Your name?" the guard asked.

"Randall Watson."

Gina noticed another uniformed guard, this one younger looking, come out of a nearby building and walk over to stand between the booth and the Lexus, just beside the gray-haired guard. He said nothing as the first guard again glanced down at the clipboard, but he leaned over a bit so he could look into the car. He smiled at her, and she smiled back. One thing she would say about Rossmoor, they did have security.

Finally the gray-haired guard shook his head. "I'm sorry, Mr. Watson. Mr. Longman hasn't put you on the guest list. Would you like me to call and let him know you're here?"

"If you'll just tell me how to find his place—"

"I'm sorry, sir," the younger guard said, cutting him off. "We need to have the resident's permission before we let anyone pass. I'm sure you understand," he said pleasantly. "It's for security reasons."

Sighing in frustration, Randall gave in. "All right. Call him." Shaking his head, he looked at Gina. "This place is harder to get into than Fort Knox."

"Well, it should make you feel better to know that once your grandmother's living here, she'll be safe."

"My grandmother is not going to be living here," Randall said firmly, and looked forward.

Gina didn't argue. For nearly an hour she'd been arguing that his grandmother was a grown woman and that he wouldn't accomplish anything if he went storming into Jack Longman's house, ranting and raving. Obviously her words hadn't had any effect. Randall Watson looked like a man on the warpath.

"I'm sorry, sir. There's no answer," the gray-haired guard said, hanging up the phone.

"What do you mean, there's no answer?" Randall leaned his head slightly out the window. "He's got to be there. My grandmother came to see him. She would have arrived just a short while ago. He's got to be there—she's got to be there—and I've got to see them *now*."

As Randall's voice rose, Gina could see both guards pulling back, their smiles disappearing. She also noted that Randall was clenching the steering wheel, his knuckles turning white. Putting a hand on his, she leaned across the seat so she could speak out the window. "We're concerned something might have happened to her...to both of them," she said sweetly, again smiling at the younger guard.

Her words seemed to have the desired effect. The gray-haired guard again looked at his clipboard. "What was her name?"

"Ella Flemming," Gina said.

He nodded. "Yep, she arrived at 8:30 this morning."

"So where is she now?" Randall demanded.

"Tell you what I'll do," the younger guard said, ignoring Randall and speaking to Gina. "I'll go check. I'm sure there's nothing to be concerned about. Could be they just stepped outside and didn't hear the phone."

"We'd appreciate that," Gina said, hoping Randall wouldn't say anything more.

To her relief, he kept quiet, but he glanced her way, lifting an eyebrow ever so slightly. Sitting back, she pulled her hand away from his and shrugged. "Sorry I interrupted, but they didn't seem to be responding very well to being yelled at."

"I wasn't yelling," he said tightly.

She didn't contradict him, but merely smiled. He made a grumbling sound, then leaned back himself. Then he looked at her, frowning. "Do you flirt with every man who comes along?"

"Flirt?" His question surprised her. "I wasn't flirting."

Randall grunted.

"The man's gotta be in his fifties." She crossed her arms in front of her chest defensively and glared at him. "Besides, he smiled first."

Again Randall grunted, looking away from her and out the front window. She could say what she liked, but she was a flirt, smiling all the time and being friendly. Why he found her attractive, he didn't know. He didn't like flirts.

And he didn't like pushy women who stuck their noses where they didn't belong.

He had to admit, however, that by butting in Gina had probably stopped him from getting himself kicked off the premises. He knew better than to yell at those guards. They were only doing their job. But, damn it, his job was to keep his grandmother safe. He'd promised his grandfather he would watch over her, take care of her.

It seemed an eternity that they had to sit where they were, doing nothing. Irritated, Randall was on edge when the younger guard drove back. Instead of getting out of his car and coming right over, the guard waited for a white Cadillac to pull into the parking spot beside him.

A white-haired woman got out of the Cadillac, and the guard walked with her toward Randall's Lexus. "This is Jack Longman's neighbor," he said when he reached the window. "Helen Tank. She says she talked to Jack and your grandmother this morning. She knows where they've gone."

"Gone?" Randall looked at the woman who'd approached his car. She was as old as his grandmother, if not older, and she had alert blue eyes and a warm smile. Her smile grew wider when she leaned over to look into the car.

"They've gone to Lake Tahoe," she said. "You must be Ella's grandson. She said you might come here. She said to tell you not to worry, that she knows what she's doing. Your grandmother is a lovely lady."

"Lake Tahoe?" Randall repeated. That was at least a three-hour drive.

"They're going to Jack's place," Helen explained, and glanced over at Gina. "They're getting married up there at one of those wedding chapels. After all these years. Isn't it romantic?"

Randall didn't have to look to know that Gina was agreeing. Why was it women always thought marriage was romantic? Even his mother, after two disastrous marriages, had jumped into another bad one. Thank goodness, he had a more realistic opinion of the institution. "When did they leave?"

Helen glanced at her wristwatch. "About an hour ago, I'd say."

An hour. That wasn't too much of a head start, Randall decided. Jack Longman was the same age as his grandmother. Despite how little he'd actually listened, it seemed to Randall that his grandmother had said something about Jack having been wounded in the leg when he was in the war. The guy probably had arthritis. Probably would drive slowly. Most old people did. All he would have to do, Randall figured, was push the speed limit and he could make up the time difference. He could easily get to Lake Tahoe in time to stop his grandmother from making a big mistake. "Where is this place of his?" he asked the woman standing beside his car.

"I'm not sure," she said, shaking her head. "South Shore, I think. Or somewhere around there. My husband knows but he's at an aviation meeting right now. He should be back in about an hour. You could ask him."

Randall knew he couldn't waste an hour. He looked at Gina. "Do you know where this place is?"

"No. He sent some pictures that showed his house and the lake, but I don't think he ever gave an address."

Randall turned back to Helen. "You're sure his place is on the south shore of the lake?"

"Pretty sure," she said, sounding hesitant. "To be honest, I never paid that much attention, but I know my husband could tell you." Again she glanced at her watch. "I'm sure he'll be back in an hour."

"I'm afraid I can't wait that long." An hour might be too late. Randall started the car. If he was going to stop a wedding, he had to get going.

He did remember to thank the woman—and the guard who'd brought her to the gate. Then he turned his car around and started for the freeway. Only later did he wish he'd given Helen his cellular phone number. A call from her husband would have made finding Jack Longman so much easier.

As Randall drove away from the entrance to Rossmoor, Gina hoped he'd finally come to terms with what his grandmother was doing. It wasn't until they reached the freeway that she understood why he wasn't grumbling or complaining. Instead of taking the freeway back the way they'd come, Randall turned onto the ramp taking them toward Sacramento...and Lake Tahoe. "What are you doing?" she asked immediately.

"Going after my grandmother."

"You can't chase her all over the country."

"I'm not going to chase her all over the country. I'm driving to Lake Tahoe." He glanced at the clock on the dashboard. "With luck, we can cut the time difference down to nothing."

"And when we get to Tahoe?"

"We talk my grandmother into forgetting this foolishness."

Beside the fact that she didn't see the elopement as foolish, Gina figured they had a bigger problem. "What do you think Jack and Ella are going to do? Stand in the middle of the highway and flag us down? I've spent a fair amount of time around the lake. Even focusing on the South Shore area, we're talking a lot of shoreline and a lot of houses.

Finding Jack Longman's place isn't going to be all that easy.''

"Someone up there will know where the guy lives. Someone at the post office. At a gas station...grocery store.''

Gina sank back against the seat. The man was impossible. Talk about single-minded. He just wasn't going to let this drop.

But that didn't mean she wanted to be a part of the situation. "Look, if you're so determined to go after your grandmother, fine, but take me back to Los Altos. I'm not going with you.''

"You've got to,'' he said, shooting her a quick glance. "I need your help.''

"*My* help? How can *I* help you?'' She was as much in the dark about this as he was.

"You said Jack sent pictures of his cabin.''

"Yeah, but if they showed a street sign or the house number, I don't remember it. All he wrote was that he and his wife used to go up to Lake Tahoe every summer, and that he loved the area.''

"He must have said what area.''

"If so, I'm drawing a blank.''

"Try to remember.''

"I am,'' she snapped, and closed her eyes. She tried to picture the area. "On the south shore there's Bijou and Stateline. Kingsbury. Round Hill Village. Zephyr Heights.'' Her eyes flew open. "That's it. I do remember him mentioning Zephyr Cove. He lives somewhere near Zephyr Cove.''

"Good.'' Randall nodded. "Then Zephyr Cove is where we'll start asking questions. And since you've seen the pictures of his house, you just might recognize it if we should drive past it.''

"In other words, you're going to drag me up there whether I want to go or not?" She didn't wait for his reply. She knew the answer. "That's going to take all day. Maybe part of the night."

"So I'll pay you overtime."

She sighed in frustration. "It wasn't the money I was worried about."

"Then what?" He frowned, then seemed to find his own answer. "Ah, yes, the boyfriend."

That took her by surprise. "What boyfriend?"

"The one I met at that play we both attended." He looked her way, then back at the road. "

"Oh... You mean Tom."

Gina remembered the night Randall had met Tom Newburry. It was the first Saturday in December. At the last minute, she'd asked Tom to go with her to a play being performed at De Anza College.

During the intermission as they stood in the lobby, she'd tried to explain to Tom the symbolism in the stage setting. She was making a big circle with her right hand, to point out how the ring on stage stood for the circle of life, when she saw Randall across the room with a drop-dead blonde, who had legs to her chin and one of those figures she'd thought only Barbie dolls possessed. Randall must have thought she was waving him over, because he nodded and started toward her, the blonde by his side.

"Well, this is a surprise," he said, giving her the usual lift of his eyebrows. "I thought my grandmother said you were going to be out of town this weekend."

"Change in plans," Gina explained. "The gal I was going to Monterey with got ill yesterday."

She began introducing Tom to Randall, but stopped when she noticed that Tom's gaze was locked on the blonde's chest, his eyes nearly bugging out. Not that Gina could really blame Tom. The blonde's sleek black dress exposed more than it covered, and Tom had always appreciated a nice set of breasts. Gina wasn't sure, however, how Randall was going to react to another man ogling his date.

When she'd looked at him, Randall was frowning, as she expected. But instead of saying something, he gave Gina an equally assessing look, letting his gaze drift down over her outfit.

Because it was so close to Christmas, she'd worn dangly red earrings and a sparkly red tunic. It hung, untucked, over a pair of black leggings. Combined with her black boots, the outfit was comfortable, but certainly not sophisticated or sexy. Sexy required long legs, which she didn't have, and sexy required a bustline that was above average. Hers showed no exaggerated protrusions in front. Certainly nothing to capture Randall's attention. He quickly looked back at her face, then over at Tom.

Who was still gaping at the blonde.

Gina poked Tom, trying to get his attention. She should have looked first to see if he'd finished his drink.

He hadn't.

Her elbow hit his arm, jostling the hand that was holding the plastic cup of soda he'd purchased at the start of the intermission. The liquid went sloshing out of the cup, through the air, straight onto the front of the blonde's dress and down the valley between her breasts.

Squealing as the cold liquid came into contact with her skin, the blonde jumped back, catching one of her spiked heels on the carpeting to send her tumbling down in a very unglamorous heap. Suddenly Randall was on his knees beside the blonde, fussing over her, and Tom was apologizing, and Gina wondered why she always looked like a klutz when she was around Randall.

Normally she didn't knock a drink out of a person's hand

or run into people, but this debacle marked the third time she'd either bumped right into Randall or caused something to spill in front of him. She was glad when the lights blinked, signaling the end of intermission. All she wanted to do was escape back to her seat. But once safely there, Tom had given her a hard time.

"I can't believe you did that," he'd said.

"It was an accident," she'd argued.

"You were jealous."

"Me? Jealous?" She couldn't imagine where he'd come up with that idea.

He'd merely smiled and said, "I'm glad." She should have known then that her relationship with Tom had changed.

"You were jealous that night," Randall said, bringing Gina back to the present.

"I was not. Tom was just a friend. Why would I get jealous? I was more afraid *you* might get jealous. I mean, Tom wasn't being very subtle about where he was looking."

"Uh-huh." The corner of Randall's mouth turned up.

"It's the truth," she insisted. "I mean, *I* certainly would have been upset if I were a man and you'd looked at my date that way."

"If that's your story." Randall's grin became a little more obvious.

"Darn it all, I was not jealous. And that's not a story. I've known Tom for years. We went to high school together. And college. If he needed a date, he called me. If I needed one, I called him. We were friends."

Randall looked her way, his eyebrows lifting. "*Were* friends? That sounds like you're not friends anymore."

"Well, it's not my fault we're not. He's the one who ruined it all by telling me he was in love with me and asking me to marry him.'' His declaration had taken her completely by surprise, and it still bothered her that he was taking her refusal as a personal affront. ''Trust me, it was the last thing I'd expected.''

''I take it you turned him down.''

''Of course I turned him down. I mean, we were friends, buddies. I liked him, but liking someone doesn't mean you want to marry him…or should. I wasn't in love with him.''

''So you're not seeing anyone right now?''

She half laughed. ''You could say I'm between engagements.''

Randall wondered why he was glad to hear she didn't have a boyfriend. It shouldn't matter, yet it did. He smiled as he passed a semi on the highway. ''You were wise to turn the guy down.''

''Why's that?''

''Because of the way he was looking at Gail. A man who's in love with a woman should be giving *her* his full attention. Otherwise, trust me, she's in for a lot of heartaches down the road.'' The kind of heartaches his mother had suffered.

Randall knew that if he'd been with Gina that night, he would have given her his full attention. She'd looked adorable. Like one of Santa's elves. And she was so embarrassed by what had happened. It was cute.

Beside him, Gina sighed. ''I wish you had let me pay to have your date's dress cleaned.''

She'd made the offer right after the accident, then again the next time he saw her. ''As I've said before, don't worry about it.''

It had been worth a cleaning bill for him to see Gail's reaction to the incident. The accident had become monumental to her. It ruined the evening, and all he could wonder was how she would react to something really serious.

His mother had certainly had to deal with things far more devastating than a stained dress. Life, he'd learned, had a way of knocking you down, so you'd better be able to get up.

"Did the stain come out?" Gina couldn't help worrying about it.

"I don't know."

She looked his way. "What do you mean, you don't know?"

"I never took her out again."

"You didn't? I thought... That is..."

He gave her a quick glance. "Yes?"

"Well, not too long after that night, Ella said she thought you'd met someone who would be the perfect mate for you."

"That's news to me." He offered her a cocked eyebrow. "She didn't happen to mention who this perfect mate was, did she?"

"No. I just assumed it was the woman I'd seen you with that night."

"That's Grandma, always playing matchmaker. I've told her I'm not getting married, but she seems intent on ignoring that little fact."

"Well, we women keep hoping. But, trust me, if you say you're never getting married, I believe you." She was through *not* believing men who said they weren't getting married. "What amazes me is how many men there are in this world who have the same attitude as you."

"I don't consider my decision an 'attitude.'"

He sounded a bit huffy, not that it mattered to her. "Call it whatever you want. I just know there are a lot of you with the same philosophy, and I'm always falling for you."

The way he looked at her, she realized she'd said something wrong. Quickly she corrected herself. "I don't mean *you* you. That is, I wasn't including you... I haven't fallen for you.''

He smiled. ''Well, that's good to know.''

She thought so, too. After all, if she had, she would be in the same situation she always got herself into. ''I just seem to attract men who don't want to get married.''

''But didn't you just say you were the one who turned down that Tom guy's proposal?''

''That was different.''

Randall shot her a grin. ''Right.''

''It was,'' she insisted. ''I'm not like you. I want to get married. I'm twenty-five years old. My biological clock is ticking. Now would be a good time to get married and start a family. But that doesn't mean I've reached the point of desperation. I'm not going to get married just to get married. I want to be in love with the man I marry.''

''And you didn't love Tom.''

''Exactly.'' She sighed. ''I know I hurt him. I wish I'd realized how he felt. I certainly didn't mean to lead him on.''

''He took it pretty hard?''

She nodded, remembering Tom's tears the night he'd proposed. ''I felt like a cad...like a hypocrite. Here I'd been telling him I was so disgusted with men who were afraid of marriage, and then I went and treated him just the same way.''

''Well, in my opinion, it's better not to get married than to make a mistake, bring a child into this world, then desert him when you get tired of the situation.''

Gina looked at him and wondered if he realized how revealing that statement had been. Maybe if Ella hadn't told her that Randall's father had deserted his wife and child, Gina wouldn't have recognized the pain. Then again, she'd been trained in communications, and the tension in Randall's voice would probably have alerted her.

He cleared his throat, and she wasn't surprised when he shifted the conversation back to her. "So what are you looking for in a man?" he asked. "Money? Ambition? Or is it just good looks?"

"None of the above," she answered truthfully. "For me, money's never been very important. I don't have fancy tastes. And since family is important to me, a lot of ambition might actually be a detriment in a man. So that leaves good looks, and I've always found what a person is like on the inside more important than what's on the outside."

"Ah..." He smiled. "Now see, in my grandmother's opinion, you would be the perfect woman for me."

Gina hadn't once thought that. "Then she'd be wrong."

"Why's that?"

"Because you and I are always arguing. Tell me one thing we've seen eye to eye on since you hired me."

He didn't answer right away, and she knew it was because there wasn't anything they hadn't argued about. Finally he said, "We both care about my grandmother."

"Yes, but we certainly don't hold similar opinions on what's good—or not good—for her. For example, I think you should be happy your grandmother's getting married to Jack, not chasing after her like some bounty hunter."

"And certainly not dragging you along?"

"You've got it."

"Maybe I want you along to keep me company. Maybe I want to spend some time with you. Just you and me."

"Well, that would be a bit mind-boggling." She laughed at the idea, the sound filling the car.

He liked when she laughed. To be honest, he liked when she argued with him but he wasn't going to tell her that.

At least she wasn't afraid to express her opinions. He always knew where he stood with her.

He was the one who wasn't being truthful. "You're right," he lied. "Bringing you along because I wanted to spend time with you would be mind-boggling."

3

"So who is this 'perfect mate' my grandmother feels I've met?" Randall asked as they sped toward Martinez.

"Probably one of your harem."

"My harem?" He made a choking sound and looked at Gina. "What harem?"

"Let's see, there was the blonde at the play." She lifted one finger. "The redhead you brought by your grandmother's house that one afternoon."

"Sarah," he said, identifying the redhead. "And that was definitely business. She's in sales, and we were on our way to a meeting."

"Mmm-hmm." Gina grinned. "And then there was the brunette who picked you up last fall when you had car trouble." She lifted a third finger.

"Simply an employee of Flemming Corporation who lives in San Ramon. Since my grandmother's house was on her way, I called and asked her if she could stop by. I have never taken her out."

"Pity," she said.

"And why is that?"

"Because the way that woman was looking at you, I'd say she'd like it to be more than a business relationship."

"Well, I'm not interested in making it more than that, and I definitely don't date employees."

One more reason not to go to work for Flemming Corporation, she thought, then realized what an outlandish idea that was. Hadn't she just told him they were totally incompatible? Didn't they always argue? Just because she found him good-looking and got a little flustered around him at times, didn't mean she was interested. Butterflies and a rapid heartbeat were *not* a good basis for a lasting relationship. Her sister's failed marriage was proof of that. And it was especially difficult to have a relationship when the other party wasn't interested.

Quickly Gina resumed listing the women she knew Randall had dated. She lifted another finger. "There was one in October. Your grandmother said you took her to a dinner dance at the country club. That doesn't sound like a business date."

"That was Gail. The same one you saw me with at that play."

"Who is kaput." She put that finger down, then lifted it again. "There was the one who called your grandmother's house, looking for you." Gina now had four fingers up. "And again when we were at the hospital, after your grandmother had the first surgery for her cataracts—"

"That wasn't someone I was pursuing," Randall interrupted. "She was coming on to me."

"Ah, poor you. They just flock after you, don't they? And what's a guy to do?"

She had expected him to laugh; instead, he clenched his fingers around the steering wheel and frowned. "Women do not flock after me. I do not have a harem, and I am *not* like my father."

She hadn't thought about his father. And from what Ella had told her, R. J. Watson's reputation as a ladies' man was not one Randall would want attached to him. "I'm sorry," she said. She'd only meant to tease him, not upset him. "I didn't mean to imply that you were like your father. I just meant...that is—" She was really making a mess of this. "Darn it all, most men would like to be accused of having a harem."

Randall gave a grunt. "Well, I guess I'm not like most men."

No, he wasn't. She really wasn't quite sure what to make of him. "You're not interested in men, are you?" she asked skeptically. Now that would be a real shame.

He glared her way. "No, I am not interested in men. I simply don't like being called a lothario."

"I can understand that."

"Do you?" He looked at her again. "Do you have any idea what my father was like?"

"Ella said he wasn't all bad, even though she never liked him."

"She sees good in everyone."

"He did produce you."

"Along with a half dozen other kids."

"But you're you. Carl and Ella Flemming's grandchild. President and CEO of one of the most successful silicon-chip manufacturing companies in the valley."

"Everything and anything I am, I owe either to my mother or my grandparents. Certainly not to my father. While I was growing up, he was out impregnating every woman he could talk into his bed."

"Do you ever see him?"

"Oh, he showed up right after Grandpa died. I should have expected it." Randall laughed sarcastically. "Good ole Dad couldn't remember my birthdays or Christmas or even to come see me when I was growing up, but once he saw that I was in control of Flemming, he was at my doorstep, telling me how much he loved me. I don't know how my mother got taken in by him. But then, she seems to have a penchant for picking losers." He grumbled and stepped on the gas, increasing the car's speed. "Must be inherited. My mother marries losers and now my grandmother's eloping with a man she hasn't seen for over fifty years."

"Are you saying Jack Longman is a loser?"

"I think he's a taker. He's taking my grandmother for a ride, and not just literally. He knows she has money, so now he's all lovey-dovey and ready to marry her. Very convenient."

"Why can't you consider the possibility that he wants to marry your grandmother because he loves her?"

Randall scoffed at the idea. "You do look at the world through rose-colored glasses, don't you?"

She resented his implication that she didn't see things as they were. "And you're a cynic."

"At least I've learned not to be taken in by a lot of sweet talk. And if this guy thinks he's going to get any of my grandmother's money, he's in for a surprise."

"Why would he want your grandmother's money anyway? He has money of his own."

"Oh, yeah. What's he do for a living?"

"Well..." Gina hesitated, and Randall glanced her way.

"He's retired now," she said. "But when he was younger, he used to race cars."

"Oh, now there's a noble occupation."

"Evidently that's what her parents thought, too. But he stopped the racing after a few years. I don't think he did all that well. It was selling the cars that made him his money."

Randall laughed. It fit. "Jack Longman was a car salesman? And you say this guy's not a fast talker?"

"These cars were one of a kind," Gina said, then laughed. "But you're right. He is a fast talker. Whenever he called, I could hardly keep up with him. Ella said he was like that in high school, always going at high speed and always ready with wild ideas. I'm sure that's why your grandmother's parents didn't want her marrying him."

"And why I don't want her marrying him." What Gina was telling him only verified his gut feeling.

"We're talking about then," Gina argued. "When he was a teenager and she was a teenager. He's more than proven himself. He made his money. And just look at where he lives. Rossmoor isn't cheap. Plus, he's got a place up at Lake Tahoe, a *nice* place from the pictures I saw. He plays golf. And he drives a nice car."

"What kind of car?" Randall realized it would help if he knew. Although he was checking the vehicles they passed, it would be easier to spot his grandmother if he knew the make and model of car he was looking for.

"He drives a Cadillac. He sent Ella a picture of it."

Cadillacs were expensive, he knew. Some more than others. "New? Old? Model? Color?"

"New. I don't know the model. And it's..." She hesitated before finishing. "A bright yellow."

"A bright yellow Cadillac?" Randall laughed, understanding her hesitation. The guy was a kook. "Well, that ought to be easy enough to spot."

"Okay, so maybe the color is a little flashy but that's not the point."

"And the point is?"

"That Jack didn't propose to your grandmother for her money. I don't think he even cares if she has money or not. And I know money doesn't mean that much to your grandmother. As she's often said, 'You can't take it with you.'"

"My grandfather worked hard to earn that money."

"And died before he could truly enjoy it."

"He and my grandmother had a good life together. He bought her nice clothes, expensive jewelry. She lives in a nice house in a good neighborhood. He took her places."

"No question about it, he did a lot for her. But, as she's told me, much of that was for him, too. He wanted her to look good so people would know he was a success. He had an image of how people should act and look, and he did everything he could to preserve that image."

Including kicking his mother out of the house when she rebelled against his wishes, Randall remembered. That his grandmother had told Gina so much about the family's personal affairs bothered him. Gina knew him as well as any woman probably ever would, and he found it disconcerting.

"Sometimes image is important," he defended, knowing he sounded like his grandfather.

Gina shook her head and sighed. "Only if you let it be."

That was what his grandmother was always saying, but coming from Gina, it irritated him. She was an employee, not family. What he needed to do was get his grandmother safely back in her house and wipe Gina Leigh out of his thoughts. She was too outspoken, too stubborn, too unrealistic.

And she was a flirt.

He glared at her.

She smiled at him.

Clenching the steering wheel even tighter, he switched his glare to the road ahead. He didn't understand why he was attracted to her, and he sure as heck didn't understand *her*. After all his arguments to the contrary, she still clung to the ridiculous idea that what his grandmother was doing was fine and dandy. If he'd hoped for an ally, he might as well forget it. Gina wasn't going to be any help.

Except she had already helped him by providing information about Jack that he hadn't known. The man had raced cars and was once a car salesman. Drove a bright yellow Cadillac. Talk about gauche.

Well, there was one thing Gina was right about. He should have listened more carefully when his grandmother was talking about this "old friend" of hers. But how was he to know it was more than talk, more than harmless memories? How could he have guessed she would run off with the guy?

Then again, his grandmother had always been a romantic at heart. For the last year, she'd been trying to match him up with someone. Actually, he was surprised she hadn't tried to match him up with Gina.

Randall looked across the car.

Or had she? What if she was doing it right now?

Gina was staring out her side window, and suddenly the thought seemed very plausible to him. "You don't think my grandmother's staging an elopement to get us together, do you?"

"Get *us* together?" Gina looked back at him, a frown creasing her forehead. "Do you think she would?"

"I don't know." But they had to accept the possibility. "Frankly, I wouldn't put it past her. Ten years ago, she worried that I'd turn out like my father, and was always telling me I was dating too many women. Lately, though, she's taken the opposite approach. She keeps encouraging me to go out, makes a big deal about it any time I mention another woman. And she has definitely dropped some hints about you."

"Really?" Gina's frown turned to a grin. "What did she say?"

"That you're a nice girl."

Her grin grew wider. "I am."

"That you're intelligent."

Gina flipped her fingers through her hair. "Not all blondes are dumb."

"And that you're a hard worker."

Gina laughed. "She really was giving you a sell job, wasn't she?"

"I believe she was."

"Too bad she wasted her breath. Right?"

"Nothing personal, but as I said before, I'm not getting married."

Nothing personal, she thought. *Baloney.* How personal could it get? He was one more of the emotionally unavailable. She was certainly glad she'd never allowed herself to fall for him.

"What if you fall in love with someone?" she asked. "What then?"

"Love?" He scoffed. "If I even thought I was falling in love, I'd take two aspirin and stay out of her bed. Look, I've seen where falling in love gets you. My mother has been in and out of love—and marriages—so many times, she makes my head spin. Now she's married to a guy who's so sickly, I don't think he's going to live another five years. He's so bad off, they had to move to Arizona for his health. She's more his nurse than his wife. She—"

"So you learned from your parents that not all marriages are perfect, is that it?" Gina interrupted. "Well, what about your grandparents? They stayed together for forty-five years, didn't they? According to you, they were in love."

"That was different. And from what my grandfather said, Grandma didn't fall in love with him right away. He said even after he married her, he wasn't sure she was really in love with him."

"Probably because she was still in love with Jack Longman. Don't you see? She loved him then. She's in love with him now."

"Or she's simply trying to recapture her past, her youth." Randall shook his head. "You know what's going to happen? She's going to end up taking care of a sick old man."

"Maybe. Or maybe he'll end up taking care of her. But in the meantime, they can find happiness together for a while."

"If they want happiness, fine," Randall said. "Let them be friends. There's nothing wrong with that. Why get married?" He shook his head again.

"Why not?"

"Why not?" He looked at her. "Gina, she's seventy-two years old."

"People that age do get married."

"She's an old woman with wrinkles and white hair."

Gina grinned. "Well...actually, it's not white anymore."

"Not white?" He shot her a quick look. "And just what color is my grandmother's hair?"

"Blond."

"*Blond?* My grandmother is now a blonde?"

"She used to be a blonde," Gina reminded him. "Ella showed me the pictures of when she was in her twenties and thirties."

"But...but—"

Gina laughed. "Randall, women do dye their hair. Women of all ages."

He looked at her intently.

"No, this is natural."

"She's a blonde," he repeated.

"And it looks good. Natural."

"She did that for him?"

"Probably."

"He asked her to?"

"Not as far as I know." Gina loved the way Randall was

reacting. The poor man simply couldn't shake the idea of his grandmother being an old woman. No wonder Ella had said she couldn't tell him what she was doing. No wonder Ella was eloping.

He kept shaking his head. "Is there anything else I should be aware of?"

"You mean like the tattoo?"

"*Tattoo?*"

He stared at her, and she started laughing. "Just kidding."

Randall shook his head once again. "Now I know why my grandfather asked me to watch over her."

"I'm sure your grandfather meant well, but what your grandmother needs is your friendship, not your protection. Randall, she's not senile."

"No, she's not senile." He didn't argue that point. "She's lonely. And this Jack Longman is preying on her loneliness."

Gina knew she was getting nowhere. "You are impossible."

She leaned back against the seat and closed her eyes. This was turning out to be a long day, she decided. A very long day.

Highway I-680 merged with I-80 northeast of Vallejo, and Randall eased his Lexus into traffic, then glanced over at Gina. She'd fallen asleep miles back, right after they'd crossed over the Martinez-Benicia bridge. At first he'd enjoyed the silence. It had given him a chance to think of what he would say to his grandmother when he finally caught up with her. But after a while, he'd missed the sound of Gina's voice, missed her arguing with him. She might be irritating, but she was never dull.

Again he wondered if his grandmother was doing this

simply to get him and Gina together. In a way he hoped that was the answer. If so, once he caught up with her, Ella Flemming would laugh and tell him it was all a joke, and he could relax. And then he would tell her he appreciated what she'd done, but it just wasn't going to work.

Oh, sure, the more time he was spending with Gina, the more he was beginning to see why his grandmother thought so highly of her. In addition to being pretty, Gina was definitely good with people. She'd been a real asset with the guards at Rossmoor. Sometimes, he grudgingly admitted, a little flirting helped. And Gina didn't limit her smiles to men. She'd been just as friendly with Jack's neighbor.

Gina also had a very pleasant voice. An asset, he was sure, for a communications major. The kind of voice a man could imagine whispering words of passion in the throes of lovemaking.

He stopped himself and glanced her way.

The thought of making love with Gina had been crossing his mind more and more often lately. Even now, as he watched the slow rise and fall of her chest, noticed how her lashes touched her cheeks, how her mouth looked so tempting, he thought of making love with her. And if he didn't stop thinking about it, the pressure in his groin was going to become unbearable and embarrassing.

He looked away quickly, willing himself to relax, but Gina gave a soft groan, drawing his attention once again. Her lashes fluttered, then lifted, and she blinked. Looking confused, she turned his way. He smiled. "Awake?"

"Yeah, I guess so." She stretched. "I can't believe I fell asleep. Where are we?"

"Northwest of Vallejo, heading toward Sacramento."

She glanced down at the clock on the dashboard, then out the window at the landscape. "You're making good time."

"Traffic's moving fast. We should be up at Tahoe before one o'clock. That is, if we don't overtake them before then." But so far he hadn't seen any bright yellow Cadillacs.

"Well, I don't know about your car," she said, giving another stretch. "But I'm going to need a pit stop, and soon."

Randall glanced at his fuel gauge. It showed half a tank. Nevertheless, he knew what it was like to travel with a woman. "I'll find a station."

Gina was glad to get out of the car and stretch her legs. She left Randall pumping gas and went inside to find the bathroom. To her relief, the facilities were clean. She even took a few minutes to comb her hair and put on lipstick. Carefully she applied the rose gloss to lips chewed clean of color.

The nap she'd taken had refreshed her a little, but she felt drawn out. She missed the cup of coffee she usually had with Ella, and decided that cleaning the kitchen, making Ella's bed, washing clothes and talking with Ella was far less tiring than arguing with Randall.

He was acting like a chauvinist, and he didn't even realize it. How like a man to think he had to go after a woman and save her from her folly. She and Ella had often talked about Randall's overprotective attitude. They'd agreed it was nice to know there was a man around, someone who could be a protector if and when necessary, but they also believed there needed to be a switch on men, something that could be turned off when that protective nature wasn't needed or became overbearing.

Gina stared into the mirror and frowned. What if Randall was right? What if Ella was staging this elopement just to bring them together? Ella did have a romantic streak in her.

And she had been talking about Randall a lot lately, mentioning his positive attributes and stating it was time for him to get married.

Could she be doing this for them?

"No." Gina shook her head and put away her lipstick. Ella might be a romantic, but she wasn't a fool. She had to realize the two of them were totally mismatched. There was only one reason Ella was eloping. She was in love with Jack.

Satisfied that she looked presentable, Gina opened the bathroom door and stepped out...straight into Randall's arms.

4

Randall gave a gasp when her body hit his, and he automatically grabbed Gina by the shoulders. Still, her forward motion made him take a step back, and he found himself drawing her closer.

The sound that came from her was a combination of grunt and squeal. Definitely an expression of surprise.

He was surprised himself, not just from the collision of their bodies, but also by how good she felt in his arms. He couldn't stop himself from sliding his hands down her back and snuggling her closer. Her coat and his jacket kept it from being an intimate gesture, yet he still felt her warmth and softness. The scent of her perfume teased his senses and played with his imagination. He looked down at her face, noticed her parted lips, and suddenly wanted to press his mouth against hers. How would she taste? he wondered. Would she respond?

In her eyes, darkened by the widening of her pupils, he saw her own questions and perhaps a flicker of desire. She said nothing, merely stared at him, her breathing irregular and shallow. Again, his gaze played over her mouth, and then the reality of what he was thinking and the ramifications a kiss would have on their relationship hit him. Coming to his senses, he released his hold and took a step back. ''Do you always come out of a room going sixty miles an hour?'' he asked, straightening his jacket and brushing a bit of imaginary lint from the sleeve.

"I didn't...I mean—'' The color in her cheeks deepened, a blush adding to her natural beauty, and she stopped stammering and looked away.

Her inability to articulate an excuse amused him. Finally he had found a way to make Gina speechless. The problem was, he'd lost his ability to think straight. As much as he wanted to laugh and make a joke of what had happened, he couldn't shake the desire to reach out and draw her back into his arms, to touch his lips against her heated skin and cool it with a kiss, or at least to bask in her warmth.

Being close to Gina was dangerous. Holding her in his arms had been almost lethal. He'd come close to kissing her. Still had the desire. He knew he had to escape. If he didn't, he would really make a fool of himself. Quickly he turned away and walked toward the cash register.

Gina stood where she was, unsure if her legs would work. Her knees felt as if they might buckle, and she reached out and placed a hand on one of the display racks, needing the extra support. The saying, Nice to run into you, jumped into her thoughts, but she knew *nice* wasn't the right word. *Traumatic. Unnerving. Breathtaking.* All better described the experience.

He'd held her in his arms and had looked deep into her eyes. And what had he seen? she wondered. What had made him glance at her lips and lick his own? She doubted he even knew he had.

"You coming?'' he asked, and she realized he'd paid and was facing the door. He was ready to move on, and she was remembering their brief embrace, struggling to understand the feelings swirling through her.

This is why I couldn't marry Tom, she told herself. In all the time she'd known Tom, she'd never been this shaken by a touch or confused by a look. Over the years, he'd often held her in his arms, had even kissed her on occasion. Not once had her legs gone rubbery or her pulse exploded. Not once had her brain turned to mush. Tom had been a good friend, nothing more.

How ironic.

How sad.

Randall walked out of the station and she followed, too dazed to remember that she had intended to buy a coffee. Back in the car, she buckled herself in and looked out the side window, hoping Randall wouldn't say anything more about the incident. To her relief, he didn't.

"I was thinking," he said, "maybe we can get this Jack fellow's Lake Tahoe number." Randall flipped up the lid on the console between them and motioned toward the cellular phone resting inside. "You could try information. If you do get a number, we could...talk to my grandmother."

"Sounds like a good idea," she said. Not that she thought anything he had to say was going to change Ella's mind, but Ella might be able to convince Randall that chasing after her wasn't necessary. Gina was ready to go home. Being in Randall's presence for such a prolonged time was unnerving. He had all of her senses out of kilter.

Once she had a dial tone, she punched in the numbers for information, then gave the operator Jack Longman's name and a possible location. For a moment, she thought the operator might be difficult, and Gina would have understood completely. She was asking the woman to give her a phone number when she didn't even know for sure what town Jack lived in. And Longman wasn't that unusual a name. Nor was Jack. There might be dozens in Nevada.

The longer they talked, however, the more Gina could feel the operator's cooperation and interest in the problem. And Gina wasn't above stretching the truth. "We need to get in touch with him,'' she said. ''He has a guest with him who's had some medical problems, and we need to get a message to her.''

Randall glanced her way and smiled, and she shook her head and wondered how he'd sucked her into acting as his foil. From the beginning she'd been against going after Ella, and here she was helping him track her down. Gina might have hung up if the operator hadn't responded at that moment with two possible numbers. Gina groped for a pen and a scrap of paper, and quickly wrote the numbers down.

''Got something,'' she said, clicking the phone off before looking at Randall. ''There's a J. Longman and a John Longman. And since Johns are sometimes called Jack, that could also be him.''

''Good work. Now it's merely a matter of elimination.''

It disturbed Gina that his approval of her efforts pleased her. She didn't want to care what he thought. Shouldn't care.

Randall glanced at the clock, then at her. ''I doubt they've made it up there yet, but why don't you give those numbers a try. If we can eliminate one, we'll be ahead of the game.''

''Please?'' she prompted. If he was going to treat her like a secretary, she at least expected him to be polite.

For a moment, he said nothing, then he smiled as he exaggerated the word. ''Please.''

Gina nodded and dialed the first number. She counted as the rings went unanswered. On the tenth ring, she hung up. ''No answer.''

''Which tells us nothing. Or maybe it does. Try the other number.'' Almost immediately, he added. ''Please.''

She did, with the same results. ''Nothing,'' she said and disconnected.

As she placed the phone back in the console, she thought

of another possibility. "You do realize that Jack and Ella might not go to his place right away, don't you? They might go directly to a wedding chapel."

She could tell from the way his hands tightened around the steering wheel that Randall hadn't thought of that possibility. His look was questioning. "Wouldn't they need a license first? Isn't there some kind of waiting period?"

"I don't know. I've never looked into getting married in Nevada, but you do always hear about Nevada's quickie weddings."

"All states should have some kind of marriage regulations," he grumbled. "Something that would make people stop and think before they acted foolishly."

"Ah, but when you're in love, who wants to wait."

Again he grumbled, and she knew she was being mean, that he was truly worried about his grandmother. Gina tried to buffer her statement. "Then again, they might want to go to Jack's place first to freshen up."

"Right." He jumped on the idea. "And we're not talking young people here. Grandma takes naps in the afternoon."

Gina shook her head. "Why is it you always think that?" She just couldn't convince him that Ella was still a vital woman. "Sometimes she does, sometimes she doesn't."

His glare indicated that wasn't what he wanted to hear. "Okay, maybe she doesn't take a nap every day, but this is a long drive. And she had to have gotten up early this morning. By the time they get up there, she'll be tired."

Again, he was thinking of Ella as an old woman, coddling her. Gina gave the opposite argument. "Then again, she'd be excited. You don't get married every day."

"My grandmother is *not* getting married. Besides, we may still catch up with them before they even get to Tahoe."

Gina glanced at the speedometer. While they were talking, Randall had been stepping down on the accelerator. The car was now going faster than the posted limit. With a light, persistent drizzle falling and the pavement already wet, breaking the speed limit to catch up with Jack and Ella didn't seem like a good idea to Gina. "What are you trying to do, turn this car into an airplane? Should I make sure my seatback is upright and my tray table stowed?"

He didn't smile. "We've got to make up an hour. More than an hour, since we stopped at that gas station."

"Sorry if I've put you behind schedule, but getting us into an accident won't help."

"We're not going to get into an accident."

She had to admit, the car was handling well and traffic was flowing along the freeway at a decent clip. Still, she felt uncomfortable going as fast as they were. She found herself clenching the side of her seat and watching the cars ahead, her foot poised to slam on an imaginary brake. Only by chance did she glance into the sideview mirror. She couldn't stop herself from smiling. "I think there's someone else who feels you're going too fast," she said.

"Who?" Randall asked sharply, his concentration on the road ahead.

"That car with the flashing lights behind us."

Gina felt the car slow as Randall glanced into his rearview mirror. She didn't catch exactly what he said, and she didn't ask him to repeat it. His body language was enough to tell her the meaning. She wiped the smile from her face, sat quietly in her seat as Randall steered the car onto the shoulder of the road. Throughout the entire incident, she remained quiet, only giving the officer a pleasant smile, nothing more, when he leaned down and looked inside the car.

For some time after they pulled back onto the freeway, the speeding ticket stuffed into the glove compartment,

Gina said nothing. It was Randall who spoke first. "Go ahead. Say it."

"There's nothing to say."

He huffed, and she fought the grin she was suppressing. Again he huffed, then sighed. "Just my luck he had to be behind me."

"Better a ticket than an accident."

"There wouldn't have been an accident."

"Ah, so now you know the future. Are you always so sure you're right about everything?"

He gave her a strange look. "I only wish."

"You certainly seem convinced that you're right about your grandmother. Tell me something, Randall, have you ever been in love?"

She didn't really expect him to answer. She wasn't even sure why she'd asked, except he certainly didn't seem to understand how a person in love might act.

To her surprise, he did answer. "I once harbored the delusion that I was in love. I'm surprised my grandmother didn't tell you all about it."

"If you're referring to your engagement, she did mention it. But she said that was years ago, and that you broke it off. She said you told her that you'd never been in love with the woman, had just thought a wife would be good for your image. But as the wedding date got closer, you realized you couldn't go through with it. Are you now telling me that you were in love with that woman?"

"Does it matter?"

"I don't know. Maybe." It might answer some questions she had. "For instance, I can understand how your father using women and your mother getting hurt every time she gets involved with a man could sour you on marriage, but it doesn't seem like that would be enough to turn you completely off love."

"And you need answers, right?"

"Look at it from my point of view. You're dragging me along in *your* pursuit of your grandmother. I think I deserve to understand why you can't simply accept that Jack might be in love with Ella, and vice versa. I think I deserve to know what has soured you on love. Was it that broken engagement?"

"Let's say that incident opened my eyes as to how anyone can be manipulated."

"Anyone, meaning even you?"

"Yes, even me."

Gina had twisted in her seat so she was nearly facing him. Admitting to her that he'd made a mistake wasn't easy. Especially that mistake. Though the years had taken away the sting, the truth was he had been in love with Maureen. Head over heels in love. Foolishly in love. He doubted he would ever fully recover from her deception.

"Tell me what happened," Gina said softly.

"There's nothing to tell," he lied. "It was lust, not love. When I realized that, I broke off the engagement."

Her frown said she didn't believe him. It didn't matter, he told himself. She could think whatever she liked.

Except he realized it did matter, and he did want to tell her. "Okay." He kept his eyes straight ahead. "You want the truth? The truth is, I broke off the engagement because I discovered she wasn't in love with me, that the whole engagement bit was a sham. She was using me, getting information from me, then passing it on to one of our competitors. She never intended to marry me."

"Oh, God. That had to hurt."

It had more than hurt. "I couldn't believe it when I first made the connection." He still remembered the day he'd stopped by Maureen's apartment unexpectedly to take her out to dinner and started thumbing through the papers on her coffee table while she changed. "I found notes she'd made of conversations we'd had. I'd thought she was simply interested in my work, but these notes were too detailed to be mere reminders. So I hired a detective, had her followed. The report I received was not what I'd wanted to hear. Maureen was making quite a bit of money off the information she was getting from me. This was back when the computer industry was in fierce competition and Flemming Corporation was on the cutting edge in the manufacturing of chips. Information about a new product was a valuable commodity."

"You confronted her with what you knew?" Gina's voice was soft, and a glance at her face showed her compassion.

"I had her stop by my office. Showed her the evidence I had."

"And what did she say?"

"She denied it at first. Then, when she realized her lies weren't going to work, she pulled off my ring, threw it on my desk and told me she was glad the farce was over."

"She never was in love with you."

Gina made it a statement, not a question. She'd summed it up perfectly. "The problem is, I thought she was. So, see when it comes to love, I'm no wiser than my mother."

"Except in your case, you've become embittered and have sworn off marriage."

"*Wiser* is the word I would use."

"All right, I'm not going to argue with you about whether or not you're right or wrong, but you do have to realize there's no correlation between what happened to you and what your grandmother is doing. Jack loved your grandmother fifty years ago or so. He wanted to marry her back then. It was her parents who put a stop to it—that and the war. Jack was drafted right near the end. Almost made it through without going overseas. But then he got the orders. In his letters to her, I read how often he thought of her while he was overseas. And then, when he was wounded—"

"I think I remember that," Randall said. "He was shot in the leg or something like that, right?"

Gina smiled. "Something like that. He was in a minefield and the guy in front of him stepped on one. Jack suffered a concussion and his leg was nearly blown off. Ella said he spent months in a hospital and was in a coma part of that time. She didn't know where he was or what had happened, not until he called her. Problem was, by then it was too late. With no contact from him, she thought he'd forgotten her or was dead, and she'd met and married your grandfather. When Jack finally called her, she was pregnant with your mother. So don't *you* see, he did love her then, and he never stopped loving her. Circumstances kept them apart. He's not like your father or Maureen. Jack is a nice guy. And you're being too protective."

"I am not being too protective." She made it sound like a fault. "I just don't want her hurt."

"Neither do I. But I think you are going to hurt her if you confront her like a raging bull and try to drag her away from Jack." With a sigh, she sat back. "Do you remember that day she had her first cataract surgery?"

Randall wasn't sure what Gina was getting at. Cautiously he said, "Yes."

"Remember how you wanted me to take her home and put her to bed?"

He remembered. Gina had argued that he was being too protective then, that his grandmother was a lot stronger than he was giving her credit for. He also remembered how the incident had turned out. "Okay, so you were right that time."

"Can this be?" Gina asked, mocking surprise. "Randall Watson admits I am right sometimes?"

He grumbled a response and let his mind drift back in time. He had thought his grandmother should be in bed. After all, the doctor had just operated on her eye. But the doctor had sided with Gina and his grandmother, saying she merely needed to take it easy and wear the protective metal eye shield over her eye for twenty-four hours.

Nevertheless, Randall had insisted that Gina stay with his grandmother that night. He would have himself, if he hadn't had an important dinner meeting to attend. As it was, he stopped by the house early the next morning.

Too early, he now remembered....

Randall hadn't thought twice when he used his key to enter his grandmother's house. He'd simply walked right in and headed for the kitchen. When he encountered Gina, he wasn't sure which of them was more surprised.

She stood by the counter in front of the coffee pot. She was measuring coffee into the basket, one hand holding the measuring spoon, the other hand stabilizing the can of coffee. Seeing him, she dropped the can. Coffee went everywhere, and she quickly stooped down to pick up the can. She was still in her nightgown, and though she'd put on a blue terry-cloth robe, when she stood the sash had loosened and the front fell open, exposing a wide section of nightgown.

The gown was an ivory color, opaque, and he wasn't sure about the material, but it looked soft and satiny. The way the material clung to her body, he could see the curve of her breasts and the outline of her nipples. His gaze slid down the front of the gown, noting how the material draped against her stomach and dipped in just slightly at the juncture of her legs. His reaction was immediate. He wanted to step forward and take her into his arms, to run his hand down over that satiny material and feel her curves and hollows, feel her warmth. The desire coursing through him created a need that shocked him, and his response was explosive.

"In this house, we don't run around half-naked," he said, practically yelling. "Where is my grandmother?"

His words—or perhaps his tone—jarred Gina into action.

The spilled coffee forgotten, she pulled her robe closed, tightening the belt. Though a blush touched her cheeks, she kept her answer calm and collected as she walked across the kitchen toward the broom closet. "Your grandmother is not up yet. I'm sorry you found me in my robe, but I didn't expect you to stop by this early."

He noticed she wasn't wearing any slippers, and her toenails were painted a crazy blue color. As quickly as he looked down, he looked back up. "Is she all right?"

Gina stopped before reaching the broom closet. She was only a few feet away from him. Too close, as far as he was concerned. There was a subtle combination of perfume, shampoo and femininity about her.

"She's fine," she said. "We just stayed up late last night working on a puzzle and talking."

"Talking? About what?" He couldn't imagine what they hadn't covered in the hours they were together during the day.

"About you."

"Me?" He knew he was frowning. He also knew he'd seen few women who looked good in the morning without makeup on and with their hair mussed, but Gina looked wonderful. Absolutely adorable.

Too adorable.

"I hope the discussion was interesting," he said curtly and then turned away, moving toward the doorway that faced the hallway to his grandmother's room. "You're sure she's okay?"

"Perfectly okay," Gina assured him, finally retrieving the broom. "I looked in on her before coming down here. Her breathing was normal. Relaxed."

He wished he could relax. He felt jumpy and irritable and ready to take flight. And watching Gina, broom in hand, walk back to the spilled coffee grounds wasn't helping his mood. "Are there any grounds left in the can?"

She glanced into the can. "It's half-full."

"Good," he grumbled. "Then make enough coffee for me to have some, too."

"Oh, yes, sir!"

She lifted the broom in a half salute, and he knew she was mocking him. Grumbling his frustration, he turned and walked out of the kitchen.

Upset, as well as concerned, Randall headed down the hallway to his grandmother's room. The door was closed. For a moment, he considered opening it and checking on her condition. It was his childhood upbringing, however, that kept him from turning the knob. His mother had taught him a closed door meant stay out.

He slowly walked back to the kitchen and sat at the table. The spilled coffee grounds had been swept up, the coffee was brewing, and Gina was now at the refrigerator, the open door blocking her from his view. Randall cleared his throat before he spoke, just so he wouldn't surprise her again. "My grandmother," he said. "She didn't have any pain last night? No problems?"

"None whatsoever," she said, pulling out a container of orange juice. She held it up for him to see. "Want some?"

"No. Just coffee," he answered, though he had a feeling caffeine was the last thing he needed. He looked out the window that faced the street in front. It was safer than looking at Gina. On the counter, the coffee pot gurgled, the smell beginning to drift his way. "She seemed all right then?" he repeated, needing to focus on the reason he'd stopped by.

"Fine," Gina assured him. "I told you she wouldn't have any problems. Your grandmother is a remarkable woman."

"I know, but—"

"No buts about it," another voice interrupted.

He turned to see his grandmother coming into the kitchen. Quickly he stood and greeted her.

His grandmother accepted his kiss on her cheek, then walked around the table to her usual spot. She, too, was in her nightgown, but the long, flowing burgundy robe she wore covered her from neck to toes. The color was a stark contrast to the white of her hair and the shield that covered her left eye. She had the look of a pirate. An aged pirate, he thought. And a healthy one. In spite of the wrinkles age had given her, her skin had a healthy glow, and Randall had to admit that she looked fine.

"Ah, yes, fresh coffee," Ella Flemming said and inhaled deeply. Then she smiled at him. "I've got to tell you, Randall, our Gina is quite a remarkable woman."

62

with her, but spend the little time we have left
you have with Gina you understand?" she said.
"No, dear, you give them a chance, and you won't tell
me."

She would. Why wait until we turn our chances off
on the side of the road. She never would have any, from the
pain, but she would think only of them soon.

"You understand that you don't need so much time with
your grandfather."

5

"**Y**ou know, now that I think about it," Randall finally said, turning toward Gina. "My grandmother really has been giving a sell job on you. She certainly was pitching you to me the morning after her surgery. 'Remarkable.' That's what she called you."

Gina shook her head. He'd been quiet for a while, and she hadn't said anything. The drone of the falling rain and the steady slap of the windshield wipers were mesmerizing, and she'd been remembering back to the day after Ella's first surgery. Dropping that can of coffee and being caught in her bathrobe without any makeup on had been embarrassing enough. Being told her attire wasn't appropriate had been irritating.

But then, Randall usually irritated her.

Even now, he managed to make a compliment from his grandmother sound derogatory. "That isn't exactly what she said. And she wasn't talking about me, but about what I'd done. She really did think my getting that puzzle together so quickly was remarkable. She said you couldn't."

Randall grumbled, and Gina grinned. She was beginning to understand him. He wasn't as self-assured as he liked people to think. Nor was he perfect. Because he'd inherited Flemming Corporation from his grandfather, some might say he was born with a silver spoon in his mouth. But there

was tarnish on that spoon. He didn't have all the answers.
"You know what I think your problem is?" she said.

He didn't even give her a glance. "I'm sure you'll tell
me."

She would. Why not? All he could do was drop her off
on the side of the road. She might get a little wet from the
rain, but she would find a way to get home.

"Your problem is that you spent too much time with
your grandfather."

"What?"

"You're just like him," she explained. "At least, from
what your grandmother's told me about your grandfather,
you sure sound like him. She said he was always sure he
was right, always worrying about the business, and always
trying to run her life. And now you're trying to run her
life. Except I don't think she's going to let you. I do hope
you realize your grandmother's changed since your grandfather died. She's changed a lot in the last six months."

"Undoubtedly because of your influence."

She was sure that wasn't a compliment. "If so, I'm glad.
It's not good to let someone run your life."

"You may think she married my grandfather on the re-
bound and later regretted it, but let me tell you, they got
along fine," Randall insisted. "She wanted him making the
decisions."

"Wanted it, or accepted it?" Gina had her own opinion.
"Tell me, do you remember how devastated she was after
your grandfather died?"

"Certainly." Randall shook his head affirmatively.
"That's why I don't understand what she's doing now.
When my grandfather died, she fell apart. He was her
whole life. In fact, for a while there, I wasn't sure she was
going to make it. Sometimes that happens, you know. One
spouse dies, then the other."

"From what she told me," Gina began, "I think for a while she wanted to die. But that was because your grandfather had left her so defenseless she didn't feel she could continue on her own. Think about it, Randall." Gina had certainly given it much thought. "Your grandmother was sent away by her parents to live with an aunt because they didn't approve of Jack. And your grandmother went. She's always let others make decisions for her, been told what to do."

"No, no...now, wait a minute," Randall interrupted. "Grandma wasn't all that docile and dependent. She ran that house. Paid the bills. And she had organizations she was active in."

"Organizations either picked by your grandfather or with his approval. You lived with them for quite a while, didn't you? I think you know I'm right."

Randall paused a moment before he answered. "Grandpa was definitely the boss around the house. You didn't dare cross him or do anything he disapproved of. But he was also a good man."

"I'm not saying he wasn't."

"He just had strong opinions about certain things." Randall smiled slightly. "He and my mother sure used to clash. After my dad took off, we moved in with Grandma and Grandpa. That lasted a year, from the time I was six until I was seven. Then my mother and grandfather got into a whopper of an argument, and we moved out. We moved back in with them when Mom's second marriage hit the rocks. That lasted only six months. Not that I didn't see my grandparents other times. I used to spend summers with them."

"And when did you start working at Flemming?" Gina asked.

"When I was sixteen. Just part-time at first, but Grandpa

said he started working when he was sixteen and there was no reason why I shouldn't. He started Flemming from scratch, you know," Randall said proudly. "He always said he was lucky to be in the electronics business at just the right time, but it was more than luck. He was wise enough to move from the East Coast to Silicon Valley when he did, and he worked hard—darn hard—right up until he died."

Randall sighed. He still missed his grandfather, the conversations they'd had and the laughs they'd shared. His grandfather and grandmother had been so different from his mother and the men she latched on to. "For all his success, Grandpa always said marrying Grandma was the smartest thing he ever did."

"The idea of your grandmother marrying someone else is like an affront to your grandfather's memory, isn't it?"

"Affront?" He weighed the word. It was more than that. It was—Randall shook his head. "I just don't understand what she's doing. I know she loved Grandpa. More than once she told me she did. How can she even think of marrying someone else?"

"She can think of it because a woman can love more than one man in her lifetime. Your grandmother loved Jack, then she loved your grandfather. Now she loves Jack again."

"Nonsense." The whole idea was ridiculous.

"No, it isn't. It happens all the time."

"Maybe to—" He stopped himself. Why argue? They were going in circles. "This is getting us nowhere."

To his surprise, Gina didn't come back with a smart retort. When he glanced her way, she was looking out the side window, her chin lifted in determination.

He was sure she was thinking of a thousand arguments to throw his way. He couldn't stop her, but it didn't mean he was going to be dissuaded from his mission by any of them. Focusing his own concentration on his driving—all the while watching for patrol cars—he kept pushing the speed limit. He didn't want anymore tickets, but he was going to make darn sure he got to Lake Tahoe before his grandmother did. No matter what Gina thought, the idea of his grandmother getting married again was ridiculous.

They drove around Sacramento, leaving I-80 for U.S. 50. Gina let the issue of his Ella's elopement drop— at least for the time being—and stuck to discussing safe topics, the weather in particular. Rather than driving out of the storm, they seemed to be driving into it, the rain increasing and the outside temperature dropping. By the time they reached Placerville, the heater was coming on more and more often and the sky was a heavy gray.

Gina had made the trip to Lake Tahoe often when growing up. She missed the family ski trips, but her older sister now had two young children who kept her busy, as well as a job, and her younger brother was busy with college and his friends. Occasionally her parents talked about getting everyone together for a weekend of skiing, but so far it was just talk.

She loved traveling up U.S. 50 as opposed to I-80. The state highway still had a wilderness feel; the stretch from Pollack Pines twisted and turned, with steep dropoffs in places. What few towns there were were spaced far apart and often consisted of no more than a gas station, a general store, a bar and a motel. U.S. 50 was the only route that went directly to the south shore of Lake Tahoe, and when it was impassable, traffic stopped or had to go the long way around.

"I hope this rain doesn't cause another mudslide like the one in '97," she said, noticing the raindrops were beginning to crystalize into flakes.

"I just wish this rain would stop," Randall answered, his gaze never leaving the road ahead, the wipers barely keeping the windshield clear.

Twenty miles later, he had his wish; the rain had completely turned to snow. Gina noticed how quickly the landscape was changing to white, but she didn't truly understand the effect it would have on them, not for several more miles. Only when she saw the sign informing them that chains would be required up ahead, did she turn to Randall. "Do you have any chains?"

"Chains?" He gave her a questioning glance.

"For your tires. They're not going to let us drive through without them."

"They've got to."

She knew then that Randall didn't have chains. She also knew arguing with him wasn't going to help. She remained quiet, watching the snow fall and feeling Randall slow the car to compensate for driving conditions. They passed cars that had pulled over to the side of the road, and they saw the drivers putting on the chains that travelers to the mountains usually carried in their trunks, especially in the winter. Randall kept driving, saying nothing, but his jaw was clenched tight. Finally, as they rounded a curve, they saw the road block and the California Highway Patrol vehicles. Randall had to stop.

One of the officers, huddling deep in his heavy jacket, his head covered with a cap, ambled over, and Randall lowered the window. "What seems to be the problem, Officer?" he asked cordially.

The officer leaned back to look at Randall's tires. "You're going to need chains, sir."

"I'm just going up to South Shore," Randall answered.

The officer shook his head. "Not without chains, you're

not. We've got R3 conditions. Chains are required on all vehicles. No exceptions.''

"You don't understand." Randall's voice lost its amiable quality and took on an authoritative tone. "I have to get up there, and quickly.''

The officer again shook his head. "I think you're the one who doesn't understand. No chains, no go. You think it's bad here…well, it's really nasty up another thousand feet, and the weather reports are telling us this storm is going to get worse before it gets better. Do you have chains or not?''

"I'm from the peninsula area. Why would I have chains?''

"Anyone driving in the mountains in winter should carry chains," the officer answered curtly.

"I didn't know I'd be driving in the mountains," Randall said just as curtly. "This is a matter of extreme urgency.''

"Extreme urgency?" The officer cocked his head, a slight smile indicating he wasn't convinced.

"I've got to stop an elopement.''

"An elopement." The officer frowned, amusement turning to concern. "Teenagers?''

"No." Randall paused for a moment, then continued sheepishly, "My grandmother.''

"Your grandmother." The frown switched back to a grin. "And how old is Grandma?''

"Seventy-two." Randall glanced at a passing car. The snow covering the road swallowed the clank of the chains on the tires. "Time is of the essence.''

The officer continued grinning. "At seventy-two, I imagine so." He glanced past Randall and nodded at Gina. "Ma'am." Then he returned his attention to Randall. "And does your grandmother have Alzheimer's or something?''

"No, she's fine mentally. She's just—that is, she, well—''

Gina felt she needed to bail Randall out. "He wasn't expecting this, Officer, and doesn't feel it's in his grandmother's best interest to get married this way."

The officer continued grinning. "Gotta say, this tops most stories I've heard. Grandma's eloping." He chuckled.

"It's not funny," Randall snapped.

"Kinda cute, I think. And all I can say is, I'm sorry if you're not ready for this marriage, but you're also not ready for this snow, so I'm going to have to turn you back until you find some chains." He nodded back the way they'd just come. "You might try Lascott. They might have some chains for sale there."

"But—" Randall started.

"I'm sorry, sir, but until you have chains, you're not going any farther up this road." The officer straightened and stepped back from the car.

Gina saw Randall look at the CHP vehicles ahead, and she wondered if he might be thinking of breaking through the road block, no matter what the officer had said. She touched his arm with her hand, and he glanced her way, his body tensed. He was ready for flight...or a fight. She didn't want him doing either.

Then he sighed, his shoulders relaxing, and he lifted his eyebrows. "I guess we go back to that town and buy some chains."

"Sounds like a plan." She drew her hand back and let out a small sigh of relief.

By the time they reached Lascott, the snow was about two feet deep and coming down at a rate Randall wouldn't have believed possible. He pulled the car into the gas station and got out. Gas prices, he noted, were about fifteen cents higher per gallon than along the peninsula. He had a feeling a set of chains was going to cost a small fortune.

Unlike the gas stations cum modern convenience stores, this one still had the look of the stations of the past, a repair garage connected to the office area and a sign advertising oil changes and antifreeze checks. One attendant stood inside the office area, watching him. Randall ignored his overcoat lying on the back seat of his car and hurried into the office.

"I need chains," he said the moment he stepped through the doorway.

The attendant looked at the snow coming down. "Yeah, roads are getting pretty bad."

"Do you have some?"

"Nope."

"No?" It wasn't the answer he'd expected. "But the officer at the road block said you would have some."

"Did, but I sold the last set last week."

"Well, who would have some then?" Randall glanced out the window. The town was barely a block long. Across the highway was a café, a motel and a grocery store. Next to the gas station was a souvenir shop with a wooden Indian standing out front and a general store. On both sides of the highway were homes that had signs in front, indicating home-based businesses.

"Nobody I know of has any chains for sale," the attendant said. "Those that have them are gonna need them themselves, looks like."

"But I need chains."

"Should have brought some with you."

"I didn't know I was coming up here."

"Nice-looking woman," the attendant said. He'd looked away from Randall and out the window facing the pumps.

Randall glanced that direction and saw Gina approaching the office, her camel-colored coat pulled tight to her body and her steps mincing, the snow covering her loafers. She brought a blast of cold air in with her when she opened the door. Quickly she shut it behind her, shivered and then offered them a quick smile. "I was getting cold sitting out there."

"He doesn't have any chains for sale," Randall said, bringing her up-to-date.

"Uh-oh." She looked out the window. "Do they have them for sale anywhere in town?"

"I already told your husband, no. Least not that I've heard. Gwenn—she's the one who owns the grocery store—she was complaining just the other day that she hadn't gotten any in. And I know Spencer hasn't, and I haven't, and Roger—" He nodded to the left where one of the signs in front of the houses stated General Handyman. "He hasn't gotten any in for a long time. We had a run on the things earlier this season, and I don't know of anyone for miles who's gotten more in." He looked back out the window. "Not even sure you could make it to the next town down. Snow's getting bad. Could turn into a white-out."

The man was right, Randall realized. The way the snow was coming down, he could barely see the highway in front of him. A passing van kicked up a swirl of white, slowed, then pulled into the motel across the highway.

"We're not married," Gina said.

"She works for me," Randall added, not wanting the man to get the wrong impression. "For my grandmother."

"Well, married or not, my advice," the attendant said, "is get a room. It's not safe to be out driving in weather like this."

"But I've got to—" Randall stopped. It was no use stating what he had to do. He watched the snow fall and knew the attendant was right. At this rate, they wouldn't be going anywhere.

"I think we'd better get a room," Gina said, echoing the gas attendant's suggestion.

"Doesn't look like we have a choice." Randall watched the van stop in front of the motel's office. Considering how few units he could see available, if they didn't act quickly, getting a room might also become an impossibility.

They drove across the highway and parked behind the van. Gina went into the motel lobby with Randall. The car had gotten cold parked at the gas station, and driving seventy-five feet hadn't given it a chance to warm up. A couple and their three children were crowded in front of the desk. The sole clerk behind the counter, a young man barely in his twenties—if that old—with an earring in one ear and his long hair pulled back into a ponytail, was pulling a key off one of the hooks on the wall.

Gina looked at those hooks. There was only one key left. Although she hoped she didn't know what that meant, when the couple and their children had left the office and the young clerk turned to Randall, Gina wasn't surprised with the man's response.

Randall was. "You only have one room left?" He looked at her.

She shrugged. "I think we'd better take it. One room's better than spending the night in the car."

"You're sure?"

She wasn't sure, but she gave him a smile. "Why not? We're both mature adults. We can sleep with our clothes on." She'd take one bed; he'd have the other. "I don't see any problem."

Randall looked back at the clerk. "We'll take it."

"Room 106," the clerk said, taking the key off the hook after Randall had filled out the registration card and given the clerk his credit card information. The clerk also handed

Randall a coupon. "Good for two free coffees at Hazel's Café, compliments of the motel. Enjoy your stay."

Gina wondered how enjoyable it would be, considering the way Randall was scowling when he held the door for her to exit the office. "We should be on the road," he grumbled.

"But we can't be," Gina reminded him and hurried to the car.

Randall didn't respond, or if he did, she didn't hear him. He said nothing when he got in the car and drove to the parking spot in front of the door with 106 on it. He grabbed his overcoat from the back seat and locked the car, then opened the door to the motel room, stepping back to let Gina enter first.

She sniffed as she entered the room, a musty odor greeting her. The room was small and dimly lit, the blinds closed on the one window that faced the parking lot. Faded wallpaper and worn carpeting told of years of wear, while the usual motel artwork hung on the walls. Gina barely noticed. It was the bed that held her attention. Instead of two, there was only one.

The idea of sharing a double bed with Randall suddenly changed how she felt about this situation. The mattress looked far too small and seemed to dip toward the middle. She had a feeling that keeping to her side wasn't going to be easy. A person might be able to push the two chairs beside the small round table near the window together and sleep there, but she doubted that person would get any sleep...or be able to move the next day.

She walked past the bed to the bathroom, snapped on the light, and checked it out. Not that she knew what she would do if she found anything to dislike. They really didn't have a choice. It was here or the car.

"Bathroom okay?" Randall asked from the other room.

"It's okay," she answered, and then stepped into the main room.

Randall snapped on the TV. It came on, and he turned it off. "Everything seems to work. Place is old, but livable."

Gina stared at the bed.

She was going to be sharing a bed with a man who could make her tingle with simply a touch. She was a snuggler. Past boyfriends had told her she snuggled a lot when she was asleep. And sometimes she talked in her sleep. That was all she needed. Knowing her, she would say something stupid while she was asleep...or do something stupid.

She would have to stay awake. It was her only option.

"Right side or left?" Randall asked.

She looked at him.

"Which side do you sleep on?"

"The middle. But that's in a twin bed."

"We may have a problem. I sleep in a king-size bed, but always end up in the middle."

No question about it. They were going to have a problem.

"Anyway, which side do you want tonight?" Randall repeated.

"It doesn't matter," she began, then stopped herself and smiled. "The right side. That would make me right, right?"

"Okay, you take the right side."

He'd missed her pun, and simply kept staring at the bed. She wondered what was going through his mind. Certainly not what she'd been thinking, she was sure. She was positive he wouldn't be wondering what it would be like to make love on that bed. Wouldn't be wondering if the springs would squeak or if the bed would thump against the wall.

Oh, that would be cute.

She started to laugh at the idea, then Randall looked at her, and the laughter died in her throat. A shiver ran down her spine, and she caught her breath. His gaze was too intent, too unnerving.

Too promising.

And then he looked away. "I'd better call my office."

6

Randall made his call to his secretary, explaining the situation. Gina noticed that he didn't mention he was traveling with her. As far as Randall's office would know, he was stuck in a motel on Highway 50, alone.

Gina called her apartment after Randall hung up. She knew her roommate wouldn't be home, but she left a message on the answering machine. There was no need for Darlene to worry, or to have her calling the police because she thought Gina might have been abducted.

In reality, Gina knew, she had been abducted. Randall hadn't threatened her with bodily harm, but he had coerced her into coming with him, had used her sympathies for his grandmother as his weapon. And now Gina was sharing a motel room with him. She might have thought he had an ulterior motive, but his uneasy behavior vanquished that idea.

Ulterior motive. She smiled at that thought.

Randall wasn't interested in her as a woman. All he wanted was to get his grandmother back. Back to Ella's house in Los Altos and back to mourning for her husband. He wanted things as they were, not something new.

"Where are those phone numbers you got?" he asked. "The two for the Lake Tahoe area?"

His question verified her suspicions. Yep, it was his

grandmother he was concerned about. If anyone was having licentious thoughts, she was the one, and she had to forget them. "In the car," she said.

"I'll go get them." Randall started for the door. "We're not that far from the lake. They should have made it by now."

If they were going straight to Jack's place, Gina thought, but said nothing. Considering the way it was snowing outside, Jack and Ella would be foolish to stay on the road any longer than necessary. Then again, if they'd gotten to the court house before the worst of the storm hit, they might be stuck at one of those locations.

Gina again looked at the bed. At the moment Ella's situation, whatever it might be, seemed less perilous than hers.

Randall came back into the room covered with snow. He shook flakes from his coat and out of his hair, then realized Gina wasn't in the room. For a moment he was concerned, then he heard water running in the bathroom. Blowing on his hands to warm them, he went to the phone and quickly dialed the first number Gina had written down. He waited as the line rang, his gaze on the snow coming down outside. Then a sound from the bathroom caught his attention.

Gina was humming.

He smiled and shook his head in disbelief. Here they were, stuck in the middle of a snowstorm, in a cruddy old motel that had a bed that looked as if it was a World War II issue, and Gina was humming.

The woman was crazy.

Or incredible.

He wasn't sure which. He only knew she excited him and she made him nervous. Spending the night with her was going to be impossible. He couldn't share that bed.

The way it sagged, they would be lying on top of each other. There was no way to keep their bodies from touching.

If she could bother him by simply resting her hand on his arm, how was he going to sleep with her next to him? How could he keep from touching her?

He hadn't led the life of a monk, but it had been some time since he'd been with a woman. Shoot, he couldn't remember the last time he'd been with a woman. He'd had plans for Gail, but after Gina's date spilled soda pop all over Gail's dress, those plans had changed. A woman whining about a stain on her dress didn't excite his libido. Or maybe it was seeing Gina that night that had dampened his desire for Gail. One was busty, the other cute. So why was it the cute one who had preoccupied his thoughts that night? Why was it she was still preoccupying his thoughts?

Randall listened to the phone's unanswered rings and finally hit the disconnect button. Quickly he dialed the second number. The result was the same—no one answered. He hung up just as Gina came out of the bathroom, a fresh coat of lipstick turning her lips a seductive rose and her hair brushed into place. She looked alert and perky. He felt drained.

"No answer at either number," he said, looking back down at the telephone. "I don't know what to do next."

"There's not much we can do right now." She walked toward him, and he noticed her perfume. Had she put more on for him?

He glanced at the bed, then back at her, half expecting a come-hither smile. But the moment their gazes met, she looked away, and he realized she wasn't trying to seduce him. In fact, she seemed as uncomfortable about the situation as he was. "What do you say to a bite of lunch?" he asked, nodding toward the window that faced the parking lot and the restaurant beyond. "I owe you that much."

"Sounds good to me."

The walk across the parking lot was not that easy. Gina struggled against the snow and the wind, the cold cutting through her coat and crystals of ice filling her loafers. The highway was now deserted, the road covered with snow and the wind creating drifts. The only visible activity in Lascott seemed to be taking place in Hazel's Café.

Through steamy windows, Gina could see dozens of people at tables and booths, and the moment she stepped through the door, she heard the talk and the laughter. There was a warmth in the café that transcended the heat being blown out from the furnace, and the short, round-bodied woman with the smoke gray hair who stood behind the counter seemed to be the catalyst of that warmth.

"Come on in, folks," she called to them the moment Gina and Randall stepped inside. "Join the crowd. Find them a table, Lilly."

A thin, wiry redhead in her late twenties approached them. She smiled at Randall, then glanced at Gina. "Follow me," she said.

Lilly led them to one of the few empty booths left in the restaurant, and Gina felt the eyes of the other patrons on her. This was not a restaurant one could slip into unnoticed. Conversations had quieted and heads turned the moment she and Randall had entered the café. Gina smiled as she passed each table and booth.

Young and old mingled together. Some, she imagined, lived in this town. Others, she was sure, were stranded motorists, like Randall and her. The weather had brought together strangers and was turning them into fast friends. She saw the couple with the three children who had checked into the motel ahead of them. They were already talking to another family with children.

"You two get stuck by this storm?" Lilly asked, setting two menus on the booth's table.

"They wouldn't let us go on," Randall said, his displeasure clear. He waited until Gina had slipped in on one side of the booth before he slid in on the other side.

"They're stoppin' everyone," a gray-haired man in the next booth said, turning toward them. He smiled at Gina. "They say it's gonna be a regular blizzard. You two heading up to South Shore or coming down from there?"

"Heading up," Gina answered and rotated in her seat so she was half-facing the man. "And you?"

"Me and the missus were on our way up." He glanced at the white-haired woman seated across the table from him. The woman smiled an acknowledgement, and her husband continued, "We were gonna do a little gambling, but I guess we're going to have to do a little swooning instead."

"Ralph," his wife chastised. "Watch what you say. Not everyone understands you're kidding."

Ralph winked at Gina. "She thinks I'm kidding." Grinning, he looked over at Randall. "You two gonna do some gambling or are you heading for one of those wedding chapels?"

Gina saw Randall stiffen, and she started to say something, but he spoke first. "We were on our way to get my grandmother."

"You two want anything to drink?" Lilly asked, still standing by the table.

"A coffee," Gina ordered. She'd missed her morning cup with Ella and had forgotten one at the gas station.

"Same," Randall echoed then looked at Gina. "We'd better look at the menu."

"Steak's good," Ralph said. "And, Edith, you liked your pork chops, didn't you?"

Gina heard Edith's positive response. Pork chops, however, didn't appeal to Gina, not this afternoon. She scanned the menu, trying to decide if she wanted to eat light or have a big meal. It was after one o'clock...and she was hungry. She decided on a full meal.

Lilly brought their coffees and took their orders. Randall was surprised when Gina asked for the chicken dinner, then decided it sounded good and did the same. Lilly headed for the kitchen, and Randall looked over at Gina.

In the warmth of the restaurant, she'd taken off her coat. Static caused her sweater to cling to her body, outlining her breasts. She definitely wasn't as well endowed as Gail, but Gina had a nice figure. She was pretty and outgoing and all-around nice, except when she decided to be stubborn and argumentative.

"She is not stubborn and she is not argumentative," he remembered his grandmother telling him one weekend. "You know what your problem is?" She didn't give him time to answer before she continued, "Your problem is that Gina has the audacity to stand up to you."

He'd argued that wasn't the problem, yet he didn't feel he'd gotten anywhere with the discussion. "I like her," his grandmother had said firmly, then smiled. "And I think you do too."

He'd disagreed. He'd said he hardly knew Gina. And that was the truth. Even now he hardly knew her.

"You know," he said. "You've been grilling and analyzing me all morning, but I barely know anything about you."

She leaned back in the booth and smiled. "So what do you want to know?"

"Why a college graduate is content to work as a companion for a seventy-two-year-old woman."

"Basically what I explained when you interviewed me. Six months ago, Zimback's had just closed its doors and I was out of a job. I saw your ad, the pay you were offering was good, and I figured that since you were only looking for someone short-term, it would give me a chance to think about what I wanted to do with the rest of my life and time to check out some possibilities before making a decision."

"And so you applied to Flemming?" He had his suspicions as to why.

"Your grandmother pushed me into that, but I don't have my hopes up. I mean, the job does sound interesting, but—" She paused and grinned. "Let's be real, Randall. The way you and I argue, I know you're not going to hire me."

"We don't argue that much." And sometimes she did have a point, much as he hated to admit it.

She continued grinning. "Let's see…" She held up her right hand. "We argued over whether your grandmother should walk more than a mile or not." Gina curled down one finger. "And we argued over—"

Randall put down his coffee and placed his hand over hers, enfolding her fingers in his. "I don't need another countdown."

She didn't go on, simply stared at him, her blue-gray eyes growing darker, smokier, and he felt the warmth of her skin seeping into his, warming his hand. He saw her swallow, then lick her lips, and as his gaze played over her mouth, the same wayward thought flickered through his mind as it had earlier that day. How would she taste?

His gaze snapped back to her eyes, and he released his hold on her hand, quickly reclaiming his cup of coffee. He cleared his throat. "So have you applied to other companies?"

"A…a few." She sounded hoarse and cleared her throat, too. "I'm hoping one in particular will be interested in my résumé. It's a company located in Santa Clara. They're looking for a PR person. The job sounds interesting."

"And what are your long-term career plans?"

"Long-term?" She frowned at the question. "What do you mean?"

"Didn't you say you wanted to get married? Have kids? What about that ticking biological clock? The house in the country and the white picket fence?"

She laughed, the sound warm and delightful. "I don't remember saying I wanted a house in the country and a white picket fence."

"Well, whatever. How do you plan on both a career and marriage?"

"Considering I don't have a boyfriend and no immediate prospects for one, the marriage and children bit may have to wait awhile. But even if I should get married, I don't see why I can't also have a career. I'm good at what I do, and the nice thing about my field is that I can do freelance work. I could prepare speeches for people. Put together presentations. It's not that I feel I have to break the glass ceiling or anything like that, but I like working." She grinned. "I may have done some housework at your grandmother's, but scrubbing floors and polishing furniture isn't my thing."

"So, you're good at what you do." He liked her confidence. "Maybe Flemming Corporation should consider your résumé."

She gave a shrug and a half smile. "That would be up to you."

"And if we offered you a job?"

Again, she didn't give him a complete smile. "I'd consider it."

"Consider it?" He shook his head and chuckled. She was either very coy or very honest.

And if he were being honest, for him to even consider hiring Gina was insane. He believed she would be a good employee—she'd certainly proven herself a reliable, hard worker these past six months—but she disturbed him too much. She turned him on sexually, and to bring her into the company, put her on the payroll—and create a situation where they might run into each other—well, the idea was crazy. Laughable.

"What are you grinning about?" Gina asked, suddenly realizing that he'd been doing a lot of grinning this trip, and wishing that his grins didn't turn her insides to liquid.

"Nothing," he said and glanced around the restaurant.

She focused on her cup of coffee and tried to figure out why Randall had such a powerful effect on her. Just the touch of his hand a moment ago had sent her thoughts awry and stoked a fire she didn't want burning. They were opposites. She irritated him; he irritated her. Opposites might attract, but they didn't create lasting bonds. They got on each other's nerves. Heck, by the time they got out of this motel, she and Randall would probably be ready to kill each other.

To think his grin meant anything was absurd. To let it affect her was self-destructive. She had to remember who he was and why she was with him. She had to gain control of her emotions.

"Two chicken dinners," Lilly said, coming up to the table with steaming plates.

Gina was glad for the interruption.

They ate and they talked; Ralph occasionally interrupting with a comment or two. He didn't bother to hide that he was eavesdropping. Even Hazel, the woman who'd greeted them when they first entered the café, came over and talked to them, encouraging them to come in anytime they got tired of sitting in their room. "This storm's gonna be a bad one," she said and ambled off to another booth.

Ralph and Edith left their booth, but not the café. With the help of others, Ralph pushed several tables together and asked Hazel for a deck of cards. Six of the patrons, Ralph and Edith included, arranged themselves around the tables and the cards were dealt. Leaning back in his chair, Ralph called to them. "You two want to join us?"

Randall didn't hesitate in giving an answer. "No, we've got to get back to the room," he told Ralph.

Gina knew how that would be interpreted even before a chuckle rippled through the café.

"To make some calls," Randall quickly added.

The smiles indicated that no one believed him, and Gina knew the more Randall said, the worse it would get. She did find the blush that reached his cheeks rather appealing. It wasn't often that she saw a man blush.

"I do need to make some calls," he repeated to Hazel when he paid the bill.

Hazel rang up the amount with barely a smile. "Sometimes you've got to leave the office behind," she said and counted out his change. Then she glanced at Gina. "Sometimes it's best just to enjoy a situation."

"She works for me," Randall said. "Works for my grandmother. We're just on our way to bring my grandmother back home."

Hazel smiled broadly, her rounded cheeks dimpling. "As I said, sometimes it's best to enjoy a situation. Have a nice afternoon, you two."

"She doesn't understand," Randall grumbled and guided Gina toward the door.

Gina had to agree with him. If Hazel thought some hanky-panky was going to occur in their room, she was sadly mistaken. You needed two to play. Randall, Gina knew, would be making those phone calls.

Getting back to the room was even more difficult than going to the café had been. The snow created a curtain of white, and Gina could well imagine how people could get disoriented in a storm and die only feet away from the safety of shelter. By the time they entered their room, she felt as if she'd hiked Mount Everest. The contrast between the cold outside and the warmth inside made her lids heavy, and as Randall headed for the telephone, Gina headed for the bed. "I'm going to lie down for a while," she said. "I'm exhausted."

He mumbled something, and she watched him pick up the phone. She laid her coat over the back of the chair, and her loafers ended up near the wall. Stretching out on the bedspread, Gina closed her eyes. She would rest for just a little while, let her body relax a little. Being around Randall Watson was emotionally draining. She needed a brief time-out.

Randall listened to the busy tone, then hung up the phone. The first time he'd heard the busy tone, he got excited. If the line was busy, someone was home. Or so it would seem.

But after a half hour of trying the two numbers and continually getting busy signals, he began to doubt the validity of that logic. It was one thing if one line were busy. For both to be busy was too much of a coincidence. Finally he called the operator and had her check the lines. Her response wasn't what he wanted to hear. There was something wrong. All of the phones around that section of the lake were out.

"It's the storm," the operator said.

The storm seemed to be controlling his life, he thought irritably. Hanging up the phone, he tried to decide what to do next. Turning slightly in his chair, he looked over at Gina.

She'd fallen asleep, her breathing soft and deep. She looked angelic with her taffy-colored hair haloing her head and her features in repose. *An angel.* He smiled. Now that was an illusion.

What she was was the devil, tempting him with her looks and teasing him with her fire. Watching her sleep, he remembered another time he'd watched her napping.

He'd stopped by his grandmother's one afternoon early in September. He'd been in the area and thought he'd drop in and say hello. He'd let himself into the house using his key and had called out a greeting. When he got no answer, he went looking for them.

He found them in the backyard. It was an unseasonably warm afternoon, and his grandmother was sitting in a chair under the roof's protective overhang. Shaded from the sun and from any breeze, she was snoring away, her head tilted to the side and her chin on her chest.

Beside her on the chaise longue was Gina, a book of poetry lying open on her chest. Her eyes were also closed, and though she wasn't snoring, Randall knew she was asleep.

He decided not to wake them. For a moment he simply absorbed the scene. Gina was wearing shorts and a simple scoop-neck top. One month after she was hired, Gina stopped wearing traditional work clothes and began arriving in casual wear. At his grandmother's insistence, Gina had told him when he asked. Well, if she was going to dress that way, he saw no reason not to enjoy the view. He gazed unabashedly at her shapely legs, visually caressed the contour of her breasts and thoroughly enjoyed her beauty. Then he quietly left, and never told either of them about his visit. But he'd held that image of Gina sleeping on that chaise longue in his mind. Sometimes, when he least expected it, the picture came back to him, teasing his libido.

Now he would have another image to hold on to.

Standing, he stretched cramped muscles. At least Gina was getting some sleep. He didn't think he would, not on that bed. Not with her beside him. As it was, he wanted to go over and stretch out beside her, take her into his arms and cuddle her close. He wanted to kiss those tempting lips and taste her.

He wanted to make love with her.

Randall decided he'd better get out of the room.

7

Randall came through the doorway, gasping and sputtering, snow clinging to his overcoat and his hair frosted white. His cheeks were ruddy and the first breath he took came out steamy, the outside cold following him into the room. He hurried to close the door, then set down the sack he carried and shook the snow from his clothing and body. "It is cold," he said, the chattering of his teeth emphasizing his words.

Gina sat cross-legged on the bed and shivered herself at the cold he'd brought into the room. She'd been watching the news on the television, the weather bulletins tracking the progress and severity of the storm. They were in the middle of a blizzard, temperatures way below freezing, with all roads closed or closing and a listing of cancelled events running along the bottom of the screen.

"Where have you been?" she asked, not even caring that she sounded more like a complaining wife than a traveling companion.

Her attitude seemed reasonable to her. She'd been worried when she woke and found him gone. She'd checked to see if his car was still parked in front of their room. It was, though it looked as if some of the snow had been scraped off. She couldn't see any footprints in the snow, but with each gust of wind sweeping everything clean, she wasn't surprised.

She'd told herself not to worry, that he was a grown man and certainly capable of taking care of himself. And she'd told herself there was no reason for him to leave a note letting her know where he'd gone. It wasn't as though they meant anything to each other. Over and over she'd told herself to simply relax, that he would be back. And she'd tried to relax, but she couldn't. His absence was disconcerting.

Seeing him now, she didn't want to let him know how glad she was that he was back. She didn't want to sound as if she cared. Yet seeing him with his pink cheeks and snow-dampened skin, she knew she cared a great deal.

"I went to that grocery store next to here," he said. "I realized we'd need a few essentials for tonight."

After hanging up his overcoat, he picked up the sack he'd brought into the room and set it on the bedspread by her side. "I was going to drive there," he said, and pulled out a bag of potato chips and a tube of toothpaste, setting each on the bed beside her. "But it's so cold and snowing so hard, I couldn't get the wipers to work enough to see out."

"So you walked?" She could feel the cold radiating off of him.

"Not one of my wiser moves." He stopped and rubbed his hands together, then blew on them. "It's just that it didn't seem that far away."

"Here." She caught his hands, clasping them between her palms. His fingers were icy, and she rubbed gently. "You are cold."

He didn't say anything, and she kept on rubbing, trying not to press too hard so she wouldn't irritate his chilled skin. She lifted his hands, bringing them closer to her lips, and blew on them. A slight hint of resistance caused her to look up at his face.

He was staring at her, the look in his eyes deep and dusky. For a moment the intensity of his gaze held her, stealing her breath away and twisting her insides into a knot. She didn't know what to say or do. She didn't know what to think.

He moved first, pulling his hands free from hers and stepping back. Without a word, he continued removing the contents of the bag. Next to the potato chips, he set a can of peanuts, two toothbrushes and a bottle of mouthwash. Then came a hairbrush and comb.

Gina watched in silence. He emptied the bag, then began putting the items away. He'd bought food, toiletries and a deck of cards. The food and the cards he set on the table near the window. The toiletries he carried into the bathroom. She didn't unwind herself from her position on the bed until she heard him close the bathroom door. Then she stood and took in a deep breath, hoping her equilibrium would soon stabilize.

It was unfair that he could shake her to the core with just a look. And what did that look mean anyway?

She'd only been trying to help him get warm. It wasn't as if she'd been trying to seduce him or anything. At least she didn't think she was trying to seduce him.

Gina shook her head. That must have been it. After all of those comments earlier in the café, Randall probably thought she was trying to seduce him. And at another time in her life, she might have given it a try. But she was older and wiser now. No more falling for the confirmed bachelor. If she was going to do any seducing, it was going to be with a man who was interested in marriage.

"I didn't buy anything to drink," Randall said, coming

back into the room. "I figured we had water, or I could go down to the office. I saw a pop machine there."

He'd purposefully avoided buying any liquor. He knew the way his thoughts had been straying all day, and he didn't need anything that might break down his resistance...or hers. They had problems enough without adding alcohol. A simple gesture on her part—her rubbing and blowing on his hands—had his hormones jumping. He needed to be very careful, keep his mind occupied with other thoughts. "You want to play some cards?" he asked.

Three hours later, Randall knew he didn't want to be playing poker against Gina if the stakes were high. He could never tell if she was bluffing. He'd been sure she didn't have anything that would beat a full house, and what did she do? She laid down a royal flush. "I have never known anyone as lucky as you," he grumbled.

"It's not luck, it's skill," she said, raking in the pile of change from the middle of the table. "Honed from years of playing cards with my family."

"You have brothers and sisters?" He realized he didn't know.

"A brother and a sister. Andy is younger and is currently at the University of California at Davis." She smiled. "He wants to be a vet. My sister, Carrie, is older, divorced and trying to raise two kids and hold down a job at the same time."

"Parents?"

Again she grinned. "Andrew and Susan. Still married. Still sane, though we did our best to drive them crazy. Now living in Stockton."

"And before that where did you live?"

"I grew up in San Jose. My grandmother still lives there, right next to our old house."

"This is the grandmother you lived with while going to college?" He remembered that bit of information from her interview. "The one who gave you experience working with older people?"

"My grandmother *is* an experience," Gina said, laughing softly. "She reminds me of your grandmother in many ways, which is maybe why Ella and I got on so well."

He didn't like her use of the past tense. "You make it sound as if my grandmother's died or gone away."

"She hasn't died, but she is gone. She's moved on in her life." Gina began shuffling the cards, but she was looking at him. "Her eyes are fine now, Randall. She doesn't need someone to read to her or drive her places. As far as companionship, she's found someone else. I can accept that. Why can't you?"

He shook his head. He couldn't accept it because it was wrong. The idea of his grandmother eloping with a man she'd known over fifty years ago was foolish. "I've seen what happens when a woman deludes herself into thinking she's found love. What Grandma is doing is just as ridiculous as the marriages my mother got herself into. This is going to end in disaster."

"How can you say that?" The cards were forgotten, and Gina frowned. "You don't even know Jack. I think he's exactly what your grandmother needs. He's got a good sense of humor. I know, I've read his letters to her. And he's compassionate. He cares about a lot of the same things that are important to your grandmother. And for that matter, what makes you think all of your mother's marriages have been disastrous? Ella seems to feel this man your mother's married to now is just right for her."

"Just right?" Randall scoffed at the idea. "He's an asthmatic. He's practically an invalid."

"And he's loving and supportive and has given your mother the self-confidence she was lacking."

"My grandmother told you that?"

"Yes." Gina resumed shuffling the cards. "Your grandmother blames herself for how your mother turned out. But from what she's told me—and from what you've said—I'd say it was your grandfather's fault."

Randall sat back, not sure he liked the direction the conversation was heading. "And how was it my grandfather's fault?"

Gina didn't look up, just kept shuffling. "From what I gather, your grandfather never did anything to build up your mother's self-esteem. He wanted a son and got a daughter, the only child Ella could have. A daughter who wasn't as pretty as he'd hoped, or as bold. A daughter who never quite met his expectations. Maybe he never told her she wasn't good enough but a child can sense those things."

"If she lacked self-esteem, how come she and Grandpa were always getting into arguments?" As a boy, he'd cringed at some of the things the two had said to each other.

"Those arguments were part of her growing-up process. I imagine they started when she married your father."

"Growing up? Gina, she was a grown woman." He'd been the child caught in the middle.

"It takes some people longer to grow up than others." Gina looked at him. "It's taken your grandmother over fifty years to do what she wanted."

They were back full circle. "What she's doing is not the act of a mature person. Mature people do not elope." Gina laughed, and it irritated him. "They don't!" he repeated.

"Oh, you're so sure of yourself." Gina shook her head. "So sure your mother's made a mistake just because she married a man with health problems. So sure your grand-mother's making a mistake.''

"I know my mother made a mistake.''

Gina pointed at the phone. "Have you talked to her, asked her if she's happy? And have you listened to her? Really listened?''

Gina had. Whenever Ruth called her mother, Ella had put the conversation on the speakerphone, allowing Gina to hear as well. Gina had heard a woman concerned about her husband's health, but she'd also heard a woman who was happy and content. She'd envied Ruth.

"Why don't you call her.'' Again, she motioned toward the phone. "Right now. Does she even know your grand-mother is eloping?''

"No...at least, I don't think so.'' Randall looked at the phone, not moving, then he finally pushed back his chair. "Okay, I will call her.'' He nodded and grabbed the phone from where he'd set it on the nightstand while they'd played cards. "I'll call her right now.''

Gina said nothing. She dealt herself a hand of solitaire and waited, hoping his mother was home. Without realizing she'd been holding her breath, she expelled it when Randall identified himself over the phone to his mother. From that point on, she followed his side of the conversation.

"I'm fine, Mom,'' he said, settling back in his chair. "Stuck in a snowstorm, but fine.'' He cleared his throat. "The reason I'm calling, Mom, is Grandma.''

There was a momentary pause on his part, then he con-tinued, "No, she's fine. At least, I think she's fine. You're not going to believe this, Mom, but Grandma is eloping.''

Again, there was a pause before he replied, "That's what I said. I got to my office this morning and there was a message on my voice mail. I went right over to her house, and she'd left a note. She's run off with some guy she knew over fifty years ago.''

He stopped talking, and Gina could see the frown lines forming on his forehead. "That's right," he said slowly. "Yes, his name is Jack. You knew about him?"

The frown settled in, creasing his brow. "You should have told me. Warned me."

Gina wasn't sure what his mother was telling him now, but she could tell from Randall's expression it wasn't what he wanted to hear. "No," he said. "I don't think it's romantic. Mom, Grandma is seventy-two years old. She just buried Grandpa." He paused. "Okay, she buried him five years ago. My point is, this guy has got to be after her money. There's no other explanation."

Gina smiled, and moved a red nine onto a black ten. There was another explanation; Randall simply wasn't accepting it.

"No…yes…that's what I've heard." He sighed and glanced Gina's way. She smiled at him, then went back to her cards. "Yes, Mom," he said, sounding like a petulant son, then he cleared his throat again. "So how's the weather where you are? How's Hal doing?"

Gina didn't smile, though she wanted to. Randall hadn't heard what he wanted to hear, so he was changing the subject. An ace of hearts turned up, then a two. It looked as if she might actually win the game.

Randall said nothing for a while, obviously listening to whatever his mother was saying. Then he asked, "Tell me, Mom, are you happy? I mean, really happy?"

Gina waited, watching him. His face was expressive, flickering from a frown to a smile. Occasionally he nodded. He didn't look her way, but sporadically took in deep breath. She wasn't sure what was being said, but Randall was listening.

"I'm glad. I really am," he finally said, and Gina knew he was. She also knew something his mother had said had touched him. His voice was gravelly when he said goodbye, and for a moment after he hung up, he said nothing.

She gave him time to collect his emotions and kept her gaze on the cards on the table, playing a black eight on the red nine. Finally he spoke. "Red seven," he said, and motioned toward a line of cards headed by a red seven.

"So she already knew?" Gina said, moving the red seven and the cards on it over to the black eight.

"She said Grandma had told her that if things developed as she hoped, she was going to get married. She just hadn't said when." He stood and stretched, then put the phone back on the nightstand.

"I take it your mother's not upset with the idea of Ella getting married."

He made a sound of exasperation that expressed his dismay. "She thinks it's a wonderful idea." Lifting his hands, he shook his head in supplication. "You women are all crazy."

"Well, thanks." Gina didn't know why she'd thought talking to his mother might change Randall's mind. If she was crazy, then he was as stubborn as they came.

He didn't seem to note her sarcasm. Instead he walked over to the bureau and began opening drawers. "What we need to do is figure out where Grandma and Jack might be." He pulled a folder from the top drawer. "Good," he said, flipping through its contents. "It's got a map of the Lake Tahoe area." He grabbed the few sheets of stationary and the pen provided by the motel, then sat down opposite her. "Now, let's see how much you remember."

"How much I remember?" She cocked her head, not quite sure she understood.

"From the letters Jack wrote. He must have given some clues to the exact location of his place."

Randall quizzed and Gina dredged her memory for any tidbits of information she could recall from the letters Jack had sent to Ella. "He didn't write a lot about his cabin at Lake Tahoe," she confessed. "Just that he and his late wife used to go up there quite often, especially when their children were young. He did say that at one point he considered selling the place, but his children and their spouses and his grandchildren are now using it, so he'll probably hang on to it for them. He also said that since his wife died, it's been harder for him to go there. Too many memories," she told Randall. "I guess he really loved his wife."

"So if he loved his wife and my grandmother loved my grandfather, why aren't they just content to let things be? Why do they have this idea they need to get married? Why can't they just be friends?"

"Maybe because they want to be more than friends and feel they should have the sanctity of marriage."

He frowned. "More than friends?"

She laughed. "Randall, you're a big boy now. Why do you think a man and a woman might want to get married? Live together?"

He stared at her, and she knew the moment he understood what she was saying. His face screwed up into a frown. "You're saying they might want to...that they might—"

"Sleep together. Have sex. Do the dirty deed." She nodded, laughing. "Yes, that's what I'm saying."

Abruptly he stood, then walked away from the table and her. He had his back to her when he spoke. "You've got to be kidding."

"Why? Just because your grandmother isn't a young woman doesn't mean she's lost her desire for sex. It's part of the human makeup. It's there until you die.'' She studied his back. ''At least, it is for most of us.''

He glanced back at her, and she knew he understood what she meant that time, too. ''Just because I don't have time for dating doesn't mean I don't have the natural desires most men have,'' he said defensively.

She continued grinning. ''I didn't say you didn't.''

He grunted and sat on the edge of the bed, looking at her. ''So do you think they're doing it now?''

''Right now?'' She glanced at the clock on the television. It was getting late. It had been dark for a while, and after a long drive, it wouldn't surprise her if Ella and Jack had retired early. ''Maybe.''

Randall wrinkled his nose.

''You are a prude,'' she said, laughing.

''I am not. I just—''

''Can't imagine your grandmother doing such a thing, right?''

For a moment he said nothing, then he shook his head. ''Right. I mean, she's Grandma. She bakes cookies. She fixes dinner. Rocks in a rocking chair. She doesn't... doesn't—'' He laughed. ''I can't say it.''

''Because you're a prude,'' she continued, laughing.

''She really dyed her hair blond?''

''Champagne blond. It looks good on her.''

''My grandmother.''

Gina sat back in her chair. ''You know, you're really very appealing when you laugh. You should do it more often.''

''And you're very appealing yourself, Miss Gina Leigh.''

Suddenly neither spoke. She couldn't draw her gaze away from his eyes and she couldn't breathe. His voice had been a velvety stroke, a caress she hadn't expected. His look held a promise she didn't dare believe. In his eyes, she saw desire, and her stomach made a flip-flop. A warmth surged through her that heated her skin and tightened muscles. The spark that flared between them ignited an awareness she welcomed and feared.

Gina bit down on her lower lip, then rose from her chair and moved closer to the window. She turned her back on him, afraid to trust her reaction and afraid she was reading too much into a look. With a twist of the rod, she opened the blinds.

Outside the snow was still falling, turning the lights from the café across the parking lot into a veiled shimmering image. From behind her she heard the bed creak, and in the glass of the window she saw Randall stand and come toward her. He stopped only inches away, his body not touching hers, but his presence felt, nevertheless.

She waited, holding her breath. Waited for him to touch her or for him to say something. Anything. She waited, and then she took in a shaky breath, letting it out as quietly as she dared.

With the darkness outside, she could see him as clearly as if they'd been standing before a mirror. He was looking at her, staring at the top of her head. Twice he licked his lips, and she thought he was going to say something. Twice he remained silent.

The tension grew and stretched, her legs shaking with anticipation. She wasn't sure if she wanted him to touch her or if she wanted him to move away. She was afraid to let herself hope, to let herself again be deceived by emotions that had nothing to do with logic. They were two people trapped in a pint-size motel room with nowhere to go, drawn to each other by an age-old chemistry that didn't always bring about the right results. She knew he wasn't right for her, that he was like the others who had stirred her blood and promised excitement. She knew she should resist, but if he touched her, she wasn't sure if she could.

She saw him move his arm, and she tensed. He reached for her...then beyond, catching the rod hanging by the side of the blinds and giving it a turn, again closing off the outside world. No one could see them now, and she could no longer see him.

She wanted to turn and face him, but she didn't move. He was the one who moved first. She heard him step back, then away. "I'm going to go to bed," he said. "I'm tired."

8

Randall hung up his jacket and took off his shoes, used the bathroom, then crawled under the covers on his side of the bed. He noticed Gina had gone back to her game of solitaire. She glanced his way.

"Will this light bother you?" she asked. "I'm not tired since I had that nap."

"No, I don't think anything will bother me," he lied.

She bothered him.

She irritated, confused and scared him. He was a man who prided himself on his self-control. He didn't want to be like his father, flitting from woman to woman, and he didn't want to be like his mother, making the wrong choices—though, he had to admit that Gina might be right about his mother's last choice in a husband. Over the phone, she had sounded happy. Content.

It was more than he could say for himself. He'd almost lost it just a while ago. Standing behind Gina, he'd wanted to touch her and turn her away from that window so she was facing him. Had wanted to kiss her.

Almost did.

Then reason, thank goodness had taken over. Or perhaps it had been fear. He knew one kiss would not be enough. Simply looking at her made the blood surge through his body and triggered the fantasies he'd been fighting for weeks. Even now his body was uncomfortably hard, his trousers pressing against his arousal.

He kept his eyes closed and silently lectured himself on all the reasons why making love with Gina would be wrong. He knew them well. He'd been over the list many times, but tonight it wasn't easy convincing a body that seemed to have a mind of its own. Sharing a room with her made it more difficult, and he prayed he was asleep by the time she crawled into bed. He might have good self-control, but he was still a man.

He heard her shuffle the cards, then deal them out again. *Keep playing,* he willed. He needed to forget how wonderful she smelled and how delightful her laughter sounded. He needed to think about his grandmother, concentrate on how he was going to get to her and stop her from this foolishness.

But thinking of his grandmother brought him back to the discussion he'd had with Gina. He couldn't imagine his grandmother in bed with anyone but his grandfather, couldn't imagine her making love with a man. Not his grandmother.

It was…well, it was— He groaned.

"You okay?" Gina asked from the table.

Randall mumbled and caught his lower lip between his teeth. He needed to go to sleep; he needed to stop thinking about sex. He needed to stop thinking about Gina.

He was still awake when he heard her go into the bathroom. A few minutes later the light that had been shining on his closed lids went out, then he felt her lie down, the mattress giving slightly as she stretched out beside him. He didn't move and tried to keep his breathing slow and rhythmic, as he'd been doing for the last half hour. He wanted her to think he was asleep.

Minutes passed. He wasn't sure how many. She shivered,

and he heard her mutter something about it being too cold, then there was movement, and he knew she was getting under the covers. Almost immediately, her body rolled toward his, her hip touching his. The contact reawakened a reaction he'd thought he had under control, and he nearly groaned. He felt her adjust her position, drawing away from him, and he had a feeling she was clinging to the edge of the bed to counter the sag of the mattress. Soon he also heard her slow, rhythmic breathing, and he wondered if she was truly asleep or playacting, as he was. He said nothing, afraid of what might happen if he spoke. In silence he absorbed the nearness of her and prayed he would get some sleep.

The first thing he heard when he woke was the sound of running water. Blinking open his eyes, he remembered where he was and checked beside him on the bed. Gina was gone. Through the closed bathroom door he could hear her. She was singing in the shower.

Pushing back the covers, he got up.

He felt rumpled and irritable. He had slept, but not long enough. It had taken forever before he'd drifted off, and even then he'd kept waking, always aware of Gina and her nearness, always afraid he might, in the throes of sleep, do what he didn't dare do while awake.

Peeking through the slats of the blinds, he saw it was still snowing. Not as heavily as the night before and the wind had certainly diminished, but the flakes were still coming down. Across the parking lot, Hazel's Café was open and busy, a sense of warmth emanating from it even at a distance.

On the table beside him were the coupons for the free coffee, compliments of the motel. Randall picked them up and stuffed them in his pocket, then put on his shoes, his jacket and his overcoat. The shower was still running and Gina was still singing when Randall left the room.

Gina came out of the bathroom, letting the steamy heat follow her. Her hair and skin were clean and her teeth brushed, but wearing the same clothes she'd slept in left her feeling grungy. Not that she had any choice. The alternative was nudity.

She paused when she saw the empty bed. Once again Randall had taken off and she had no idea where he was. She opened the blinds and saw that his car was buried up to its hood in snow. And though flakes were still falling, she heard the whine of a snowblower and noticed a path had been cleared in front of the rooms.

The clock read eight. She'd slept later than usual, but then again, it had taken her forever to fall asleep. Lying next to Randall, she'd been afraid to move. Every time he shifted position, she'd had to grab the edge of the bed to keep from rolling onto him. No, she hadn't gotten much sleep.

When she woke, he had been snoring softly, and that had irritated her. He could sleep and she couldn't. It didn't bother him at all to be lying next to her, and it was driving her crazy. He was in total control of his emotions, and she was allowing hers to go wild.

And once again he hadn't had the decency to leave a note letting her know where he'd gone.

She grumbled to herself as she walked back into the bathroom. The minute this storm let up, she was catching a ride back to the peninsula. Randall could find his grandmother on his own. No more listening to his persuasive arguments. Ella knew what she was doing. The one who didn't know why she was along for this ride was Gina Marie Leigh.

She was brushing her hair when she heard a key in the outside door. Stepping out of the bathroom, she watched Randall maneuver his way into the room, balancing two foam cups in his hands and pushing the door shut behind him. She was ready to tell him what she thought of his taking off without saying anything, then she caught a whiff of coffee and forgave him for all past sins. "Coffee," she said with a sigh. She didn't get going in the morning until she had her coffee. "Just what I needed."

She walked across the room to where Randall stood. He smiled and held out one of the cups. "I hope you wanted it black. I remembered that was how you ordered it yesterday."

"Black is wonderful." She inhaled the aroma. "*You* are wonderful. I hope you know, I could kiss you right now."

"Oh yeah?"

There was something in the way he said the words that stopped her effort to remove the lid from her cup. She looked up at him and found him staring at her face, just the faintest of smiles touching his lips. "Yeah," she said and held her breath, waiting for what he might say next.

His gaze dropped to her mouth and lingered there, and once again, she saw that dark, dusky look—so promising and tempting. With his eyes he was caressing her, and she dared to hope. Then he turned away, and walked toward the television. "You heard the weather report yet?"

"No." She released her breath, her legs suddenly shaky and her insides quivering.

"It's pretty much stopped snowing." He snapped on the television. "But over at the café, they're saying this is just a lull, that there's another storm coming." He looked her way. "Did you see the car? I think we got three feet of snow last night."

"Looks like it." She sipped her coffee and tried to act

nonchalant. She had no explanation for the look he'd just given her, other than she didn't understand men.

For that matter, she didn't understand herself.

Randall sat on the edge of the bed, drinking his coffee and watching the television set. His hair was mussed, he had the start of a beard, and his trousers were wrinkled from sleeping in them. He looked disheveled...and absolutely wonderful. She knew it was ridiculous, but she was falling in love with him.

He shook his head as the reporter on the screen gave the forecast. It didn't sound good, and Gina knew there would be no escaping Randall's presence, not for a while. Both U.S. 50 and I-80 were closed. Activities throughout the area had been cancelled and businesses closed. The concern was for stranded motorists.

On the scale of things, she realized, her problems were small. So she was attracted to a man who wasn't interested in her. Big deal. All she needed was a little self-control. She could deal with this. She had to.

Randall rubbed a palm over his jaw, then glanced her way. "I think I'll shave, then how's some breakfast sound?"

Hazel's Café was even busier than when Randall had been there earlier. He held the door for Gina, then followed her in. Hazel was behind the counter, laughing with the customers seated there, and Lilly was scurrying from table to table, taking orders and bringing food.

"So you got her up," Hazel called to him, and waddled out from behind the counter and grabbed two menus. "Got your booth waiting for you."

"Well, good morning," Ralph said as they neared the table where he was seated. He and his wife, Edith, had joined another older couple and were seated at one of the tables in the middle of the restaurant. "You two have a good night's sleep?"

His grin said more than his words, and Randall knew what the man was thinking. How disappointed Ralph would be if he knew the truth. Or amused. "We survived," Randall said, letting the others come to their own conclusions.

He saw a blush rise to Gina's cheeks, but she said nothing. Once they were seated in the booth, she began poring over her menu. He did the same.

They'd eaten the chips and peanuts the night before, but he was hungry now. "Order anything you like," he said, his own tastes leaning toward the farmer's omelette.

When he saw the stack of pancakes she ordered and devoured, he was amazed that someone so small could eat so much. He also liked the fact that she didn't play coy and pretend to have a small appetite. He'd run into that with Maureen. But then, nothing about Maureen had been for real, from their initial meeting to their engagement.

"Stick around for a while," Ralph suggested after Randall and Gina finished eating and started out of the restaurant. "We're going to get some card games going."

"Maybe later," Randall said. "We need to get some warmer clothes. At least, I hope there's a store around here."

"Spencer's General Store across the street has clothes," Hazel said, taking Randall's money and the bill. "But don't let him hike up the price on you, honey. You tell him you're a friend of mine." She nodded and rang up the register.

"I'll do that." He took the change she handed back and started for the door.

Gina waved goodbye to the others in the restaurant as they left. During breakfast, she'd gotten into a conversation with the younger couple with the three children, who were seated at the table next to them. Over her pancakes and syrup, Gina had exchanged information on ski locations around the lake. Never having skied, Randall had no idea what they were talking about.

"So you come up here a lot?" he asked as they walked back toward the motel.

"Used to," she said. "We usually skied the north side. Squaw Valley and Incline. My brother still comes up a lot. With the Davis campus just a little over an hour away, it's a short jaunt for him and a relaxation, he says, from his studies."

A path had been blown clear between the restaurant and the motel. From there it followed the walkway in front of the rooms then made a Y, one path continuing to the grocery store and the other cutting across the highway to the gas station, general store and souvenir shop. "Shall we go over to Spencer's now?" he asked. "I don't know about you, but I'd like to get out of these clothes and into something warmer."

"I, ah—" Gina hesitated, her feet freezing in her loafers but a bigger problem looming. "I'm a little tight on money right now." She gave a small smile. "I'm about to be unemployed."

He placed a hand against her back and guided her past their motel room and toward the general store. He hadn't thought about the cost or that she might not have the money for new clothes. But really, the answer was easy. "Don't worry about the cost," he said. "I brought you up here and got you into this situation, so I'll buy you the clothes you need. I can't have you coming down with pneumonia, now can I? Hospital bills are more expensive than warm clothes."

Gina tried to ignore the shiver that ran down her spine at the touch of his hand. She might not get pneumonia, but she had to find a way to stop reacting every time he touched her. The gesture meant nothing, she told herself. She had a coat on, after all. How intimate could a touch be?

And letting him buy her some warmer clothes was appropriate, she rationalized. He was right. He had gotten her into this situation.

A snowmobile roared down the highway, another following. "For some, this snow is a problem," Gina said, watching them disappear around a corner. "For others, it's an excuse to play."

"Ralph and his friends seem to be using it as an excuse to play cards."

She laughed. "I don't think they need an excuse."

"I'll have to pit you against them in a game of poker. I still can't believe how lucky you were."

"Lucky?" Gina cocked him a grin. "Don't you mean how good I was?"

He grumbled, and she laughed.

A bell rang over the door when they entered Spencer's General Store. It was certainly not a Nordstrom or a Macy's. The floors were wooden, worn and stained with age; the lighting was dim, and the clothing was primarily displayed on tables or shelves, intermingled with everyday household items, hunting supplies and tools. The interior of the store had a musty odor and the man standing behind the counter looked to be in his sixties or better. "Mornin'," he said and nodded. "Anything I can help you folks with?"

"Warmer clothes," Randall said, heading for a table of sweaters. "Boots, if you have any."

"Get stuck by this storm, did you?" the man asked, coming toward them.

"We didn't have any chains." Randall looked toward the section of the store that had automotive supplies. "You wouldn't have any chains for sale, would you? I need a set to fit a Lexus.''

''Don't have a one.'' He glanced out the window facing the highway. ''Wished I did. You're not the first one to ask.''

''Are you Spencer?'' Gina asked, holding up a sweater.

''That's me,'' the older man answered. ''Orin Spencer.''

''Hazel said you'd give us a good deal on clothes.''

''She did, did she?'' Spencer chuckled. ''Gotta talk to that woman.'' He walked over to a stack of boxes by one wall. ''Boots are over here. Not much of a selection, but I might have your sizes.''

By the time they left Spencer's, they had a complete change of clothes, including ski jackets and pants, wool sweaters, gloves and boots. Gina had even grabbed a package of underwear. When Orin Spencer rang up the total, she cringed, but Randall didn't say a word, just handed the man a credit card and signed the slip.

Gina knew Randall could afford the clothes, but she silently vowed she would pay him back once she had a job. He might have gotten her into this situation, but she wasn't about to let him spend that much on her.

They wore the warmer clothing and took the outfits they'd slept in back to the motel room. A glance at the time showed it wasn't yet eleven. The roads were still closed, so they wouldn't be going anywhere, and the idea of spending the rest of the day in the motel room not only sounded boring, but Gina knew it could be dangerous. The space was too cramped and the bed was still unmade. They needed to do something.

''Let's check out that souvenir shop with the Indian in front,'' she said, and didn't wait for Randall's response. Opening the door, she headed outside.

The snow had almost entirely stopped, and there were

several snowmobiles roaring up and down the closed highway. The woman in the souvenir shop stood by one of the windows, watching them tear around the town. She shook her head when Gina and Randall stepped into the shop. "You'd think it was a racetrack out there," she grumbled.

"I think they're just kids." From what Gina could see of the drivers' faces beneath their helmets, they didn't look very old.

"They're teenagers," the store owner said in answer to Gina. "And one is my son." She again shook her head. "He should be studying, doing his homework. But no. They closed school, and he thinks it's a holiday."

Gina picked up an antique lantern lying on a table by the window. "With the road closed, I'm surprised you're even open."

"Never know when someone like you two might stop by. Besides, opening up is no problem for me. I also live here." She nodded toward the back of the shop, which Gina could see turned into a private residence.

"That's a sidelight," the store owner said, pointing at the lantern in Gina's hands. "Came from a Wells Fargo stagecoach. Back a hundred and fifty years ago, it was stagecoaches that used to go tearing up and down Echo Pass."

"I bet this lantern could tell some interesting stories." Gina held it up so Randall could see it. "Need a new sidelight for your car?"

"Might be a little big," he said from the table of miner's scales he was looking at.

"This is what could tell the interesting story," the shop owner said and pointed at a shredded piece of old canvas that was framed behind glass and hanging on the wall.

"Looks like a rag," Randall said, walking over to where they stood.

"Maybe so, but they say this is a piece of the canvas that Horace Greeley, the famous newspaper editor, poked his head through the time he took the stage down to Placerville."

"Uh-huh." Randall grinned his disbelief and stepped closer to the framed, tattered canvas. "And do you have a bed that Washington slept in?"

"No, I'm serious," the store owner said. "The way the story goes, Horace Greeley had to be in Placerville by seven o'clock one night. The roads were in an awful state and the driver wasn't making very good time. Greeley started nagging him about not wanting to be late, but this driver just went on at the same slow speed. Greeley kept yelling at the driver, but to no avail. And then, maybe because the road was better or maybe because the driver got tired of Greeley's nagging, all of a sudden those horses were off at a full gallop.

"Now Greeley was bouncing all over the place. He bounced so hard, his bald head went right through the roof of the coach, they say. Broke the small timbers and ripped this canvas."

"Did it kill him?" Gina asked.

"No, but when the coach finally stopped at Mud Springs, which is a few miles from Placerville, and a committee of prominent citizens stepped forward to greet the editor, the driver had to check if Greeley was still in the stage."

Randall shook his head and chuckled. "Now I know you're putting us on."

The woman looked indignant. "I am not. If you doubt me, read Mark Twain. He swore he heard the story from every correspondent who'd ever set foot on the overland road between Julesburg and San Francisco. Also, there's a painting depicting the incident hanging in the Wells Fargo Museum in San Francisco."

"And this is an actual piece of the canvas that Horace Greeley's head went through." Randall still didn't sound convinced.

The store owner grinned. "That's what I'm told."

"And how much are you asking for this *unique...*" Randall stretched out the word. "Piece of canvas?"

"It's not for sale." Again, the store owner smiled. "Sometimes a legend's worth more than money...especially if it brings people into my shop."

Gina supposed the store owner was right. Not that the story had brought them there. Or even the Indian statue out front. No, they simply needed to kill time, and browsing through a souvenir shop was definitely safer than being confined in a motel room together.

They looked at everything they could find to look at, and asked the owner questions about several of the items. She related more tales about the gold mining days, when the travelers were more interested in getting rich and surviving the winters than in skiing and gambling.

Gina ended up buying a paperweight that had a few flakes of gold imbedded in the glass, and Randall purchased a packet of postcards. In all, they spent over an hour in the shop, and by the time they left the snow had started up again, the flakes catching on Gina's hair and nose.

She slipped the paperweight she'd purchased into her jacket pocket and stooped to gather a handful of fresh snow, packing it into a ball. "You ever been in a snowball fight, Randall?" she asked.

"No." He eyed her cautiously.

She turned so she was walking backward along the path the snowblower had cleared to the motel. She continued patting the snow between her palms, lengthening the distance between them.

"Gina," he said, his tone holding a warning.

"This kind of snow makes great snowballs," she said solemnly. "It's wet enough to pack easily."

"You wouldn't dare," he said and checked his options for escape.

There really weren't any. The snowblower had created a channel effect that connected shop to shop. Roughly four feet in width, it had walls that were as high as his shoulders in places. There was certainly nowhere to hide from a snowball.

"I think everyone should be hit by at least one snowball in his lifetime," she said and threw the one she held. Randall ducked to the left, and it skimmed past his shoulder, but Gina didn't waste any time forming another and lobbing it at him. Again he dodged to the left.

With the third snowball, she anticipated his movements. The loosely packed snow hit him square in the middle of his left shoulder. "Gotcha," she said in satisfaction and slapped her gloved hands together, brushing off the snow.

He tossed the next one, but missed her, and she got him with another before he lobbed one back. When the third snowball hit him, he decided he was definitely losing the battle, and it was time to change tactics. In three strides he had her, and they went down on the snow together, Gina laughing and wiggling and twisting beneath him.

"No fair," she squealed. "Tackling isn't in the rules."

"I'm making up my own rules," he said and caught her arms and pinned them to her sides.

"You're not playing fair. You're bigger than me."

She kept wiggling, her hips rubbing against his, and he knew she was the one who wasn't playing fair. How could a man resist a woman who felt so soft and feminine, whose laughter eased his soul and made him smile? How could he stop his body from reacting when every gyration she made stimulated him?

He knew one way to stop her. Leaning close, he touched his mouth to hers.

9

Gina's lips were cool against his. Soft. For weeks, he had
fantasized about kissing her and had cursed the desires she
ignited in him. Now it was happening. He was kissing her,
his mouth slanting across hers, his lips moving with hers.

The experience was more satisfying than he'd ever imagined possible. He savored her taste, her warmth and her
vitality. The feel of her body beneath his, so small and
feminine, spurred his desire. Insanity ruled as he took and
she gave.

Instead of struggling to escape, she embraced him, her
arms going around his shoulders and her gloved hands resting on his jacket. She held him to her, inviting him to
continue and drawing him deeper into the insanity.

He probed, and she parted her lips, giving way to the
thrusts of his tongue. He discovered a moist warmth that
triggered more needs and sent a jolt of desire ricocheting
through him. The world around him was forgotten, a kiss
not nearly enough. He wanted to know her, to possess her
and be possessed by her. He wanted to experience all of
her pleasures and unlock the mysteries that made her respond, to feel her skin touching his and hear her cry out
his name. He wanted to turn her bubbly laughter into moans
of ecstasy.

She sighed beneath him, and he adjusted his weight,

making sure she could breathe. But he didn't stop kissing her. Deep in his subconscious a voice was telling him what he was doing was wrong, but he ignored the warning. Kissing her was too wonderful to stop. It was an awakening of his senses, a release of his emotions and a fulfillment of his needs. Self-denial could only be sustained for so long. From the day he'd met her, she'd been a temptation. For almost six months, he'd resisted her lure, had stayed in control. Now he was discovering he was just a man.

Just like his father.

"No," he groaned and drew back, pulling against Gina's embrace.

Snow blew into his eyes when he opened them, the tiny crystals of ice stinging cold against his face and bringing him totally back to reality. The highway was deserted. Even the snowmobilers had left. And snuggled down in the path, they couldn't be seen—not by the souvenir shop owner or Spencer or anyone in Hazel's Café. Still, Randall cringed at his actions. He'd pounced on Gina right in the middle of town, had succumbed and forgotten his vow to be different from his parents. For a moment in time, he'd forgotten everything and had simply taken.

"I'm sorry." He pushed himself up from the snow, then offered his hand.

Gina hesitated, staring at him, saying nothing. Then she accepted his assistance and let him pull her to her feet. Standing in front of him, she took a deep breath, her smoke blue eyes dark with emotion.

He knew he had to explain what he'd done. Except how did you explain insanity? He forced a smile. "Shall we blame that on the altitude?" he said, turning away from her.

"The altitude?" she asked, her voice shaky.

He shrugged, not having a better excuse, and proceeded

to brush the snow from his clothing. It was a losing battle. What he brushed off was replaced by the snow coming down from the sky. Looking up at the clouds, he tried to change the subject. "I think that second storm is coming in."

Gina said nothing, and Randall kept brushing, and the snow kept falling. Finally she spoke. "You're saying that kiss meant nothing to you?"

He glanced her way. Confusion and pain had replaced the look of desire in her eyes. He was tempted to tell her the truth, then stopped himself. The truth wouldn't accomplish anything. She was looking for love and marriage. He no longer believed in love. If he wasn't careful, he would hurt her, just as his father had hurt all of the women he'd seduced, then left. Randall refused to allow himself to be like his father, no matter what his genetic makeup.

"As kisses go," he said casually, wanting to keep the conversation light, "that one was okay."

"Okay?" She bit out the word and the look in her eyes turned to anger. "Well, golly gee, thanks."

She gave a quick swipe at the snow on her clothing, then turned and started for the motel. Randall saw the snow clinging to her back, but said nothing. He stayed a few feet behind her. He knew his words had hurt but she would get over it. It was better this way, he assured himself. He'd slipped, lost control, but now everything was all right. It had to be. To let things go any farther would be too dangerous. Self-destructive. They had to pretend he'd never given in to temptation.

He had to pretend he hadn't been affected by that kiss.

Gina didn't look back at him, but she knew Randall was right behind her. At the door to their room, she paused. He had the only key.

He slipped it into the lock and turned it, and she opened

the door. "Wait," he said, and she paused, hoping he would say he was wrong, that the kiss they'd shared had meant something to him.

"You have snow on your back," he said, and brusquely brushed his hand down the back of her jacket.

Snow on my back and the taste of you in my mouth, she thought, not moving. He'd kissed her. He'd shaken her to the core of her being, had stirred her emotions and heated her desires, and now he was brushing her off.

"I'm sorry," he said, still sweeping at the snow. "I shouldn't have tackled you like that. I could have hurt you."

She turned to face him.

For a moment, he looked at her, then he glanced away. "Back there," he said, "I...well...I don't know what came over me. I don't usually...that is...I shouldn't have—"

"Oh, shut up," she snapped. It was more than she could endure. His look showed his surprise. She should have let it go at that. She didn't. "You know what's worse," she said, hating the truth herself. "Back there I wanted you to kiss me."

She turned and stomped into the room, leaving him where he stood. Walking past the still-unmade bed, she went to the far end of the room and pulled off her new ski jacket and hung it on a hook. A few stomps with her feet and the snow was off her boots. She stepped into the bathroom and checked her reflection in the mirror. Snow continued to cling to the backs of the ski pants Randall had bought her. White against black. She brushed off all she could see, then pulled off her knit hat and fluffed her hair.

When she stepped out of the bathroom, she was surprised to find Randall still standing by the door. He'd closed it, but still had on his jacket and gloves. "I think we have a problem," he said, looking directly at her.

"Problem?" She prepared herself for a lecture. The cool, calm, collected Randall Watson was once again in control.

"That kiss—"

"Forget that kiss!" She wouldn't—never—but she didn't want to talk about it.

"I'd like to." He gave a slight smile. "There are times I'd like to forget I ever met you."

"Oh, thanks." He sure knew how to make her feel good.

His gaze moved to the unmade bed, then back to her. "Gina, we've got a problem. *I've* got a problem."

"I'm not going to jump you, if that's what you're worried about."

"No, I wasn't worried about that. But I might take you."

"In your dreams," she snapped. She didn't need him mocking her.

"Often."

"I don't need you to—" She stopped, suddenly realizing what he'd said. "Often?"

"That's what I said." His voice was tense and laced with irritation. "You say you wanted me to kiss you. Well, I kissed you. I kissed you because that's what *I've* wanted to do for a long time. In fact, I've wanted to do a heck of a lot more than just kiss you. But I know it's wrong."

"Whoa." She stopped him, then whispered softly. "You're saying that you want to make love with me?"

"Yes," he said, not sounding as if he liked the idea. "And last night, with you lying next to me—"

"You wanted to make love with me?" It was so incredible, she had to hear the words again.

"I know we're only sharing this room because we had no other choice, but—"

"Randall Watson. The man who's always arguing with me. *You.* You wanted to make love to *me*." She liked the sound of those words.

"Yes, I'm just as bad as my father."

She grinned. "Then I guess I like bad."

"This isn't funny, Gina." He glared at her. "I'm serious."

"Too serious most of the time," she said, and walked toward him.

He lifted an eyebrow. "Gina?"

"I still can't believe you're attracted to me."

"Well, believe it," he grumbled. "But this is all wrong. I don't want to hurt you, Gina. I don't want you thinking I'm offering something that I'm not."

"And what is it you're not offering?"

"Love. Commitment. You're looking for a husband. Well, I'm not looking for a wife."

"I didn't say I was looking for a husband." That made her sound desperate. "It's just that I'm tired of—"

"Men who won't commit," he finished for her. "And I'm one of them."

He was right but it didn't change how she felt. She glanced at the open blinds. "What do you say we close those?"

He looked in that direction, then back at her, understanding. "You're sure?"

She wasn't sure of anything but she nodded.

He closed the blinds, flipped the deadbolt on the door, and slipped out of his jacket and gloves. After laying them on a chair, he faced her.

Tension charged the darkened room. A tingling sensation ran through her body, anticipation tightening her abdominal muscles. She was afraid to breathe, afraid if she did, he would change his mind...or she would.

Confusion muddled her feelings. For so long, she'd told herself she was reading too much into the looks he gave her, that he didn't care. Now she was afraid to believe the look in his eyes, was afraid to trust the words he'd said. She waited as he neared, half expecting him to laugh and tell her she was a fool.

And maybe she was. He was promising her nothing. He wanted her body, as she wanted his, but he didn't want her heart. He was offering her momentary pleasure, the gratification of a sexual need. No commitments. No love.

And she couldn't say no because it was too late for her. Somewhere along the way, she'd given what he couldn't. Perhaps it happened when Ella was telling her about the little boy, so confused by his parents' divorce and his father's desertion. Or maybe it happened while she watched Randall with his grandmother, his protectiveness and love for the older woman so endearing. Whenever and for whatever reason, she'd fallen in love with him, and that love had nothing to do with what he could or couldn't give her. Her love for him simply was, and a moment of pleasure with him was better than a lifetime of longing.

"Gina," he said, cradling her face in his hands and gently bringing her chin up so she had to look at him. "I want you to know this wasn't supposed to happen. I truly thought I could control myself."

She placed a hand on his chest, her fingers pressing against the wool of his new sweater. She could feel the thud of his heart. "Some things can't be controlled, Randall." Like a heartbeat. His was rapid. "Things like feelings and emotions." Her emotions were in a turmoil. "Sometimes you have to let go and simply experience life."

He smiled. "You are an experience."

Randall tipped his head down, capturing her mouth, and for a moment his kiss held a touch of control, his mouth gentle. And for that moment, she questioned her decision. She didn't want to be a vessel and nothing more. If only for now, she wanted him involved, emotionally as well as physically.

Her doubts disappeared when he gave a groan and the control disappeared. The gentleness vanished, and he drew her closer, his lips taking on the hunger she'd longed for and the pressure of his body promising full commitment.

He kissed her and he touched her, his hands traveling over her sweater, then under it. Her skin warmed with each stroke of his fingers. His hands caressed and teased while his kisses played over her face, first branding her cheeks, then her forehead and finally the tip of her nose.

He was driving her crazy. His hands slid over her breasts and rubbed across her nipples, sending tingling messages to her deepest recesses. "Are you warm enough?" he asked, his lips close to her ear and the warmth of his breath adding to the heat he was generating.

"Yes," she said, knowing her insides had turned to molten desire. "Too warm."

"Then let's get this off," he whispered and began to lift her sweater.

She helped him, raising her arms. The sweater was tossed onto the chair with his jacket, and her bra went next, the clasp released and the lacy nylon dropping to the floor between them. His gaze dropped to her body, and she waited, holding her breath and remembering the blonde she'd seen him with at the play. "Not exactly *Hustler* proportions," she said, a little embarrassed.

"I don't need *Hustler* proportions," he said, his gaze coming back to her eyes. "You're beautiful, Gina. You look just as I'd always dreamed you would."

"Really?" She knew the question was foolish. She shouldn't care. But she did.

"Really." He brushed a hand through her hair, trailing

his fingers down the side of her face. "What's more, you're beautiful inside and out."

"I irritate you."

He smiled, then bent to kiss her. "Yes, you do. And you make me laugh and make me jealous and talk a mile a minute."

She didn't say anything when he slipped his tongue into her mouth, teasing her. And she only sighed when he began kissing her throat. The soft wool of his sweater rubbed against her bare breasts, and he held her hips against his, the hardness of his body a clear definition of his arousal. She knew where his kisses were headed, and she waited, anticipating the touch of his mouth on her rigid nipples. Nevertheless, when he sucked in one, she gave a little gasp, the spark running from her nipples through her body, catching her off guard. The top of his head was all she could see, so she closed her eyes and felt, wondering how a man's touch could send so many messages.

His lips spoke of reverence and lust, of a primal power and civilized caution. His hands promised tenderness and strength. He began to pull down her ski pants, and she stopped him.

"What about you?" she asked.

He drew back slightly. "What about me?"

She plucked at his sweater. "You're still dressed."

"Gotta be equal, don't you?" He grinned and stripped off his sweater and the T-shirt under it. Then he nodded toward the bed. "Sit down, and I'll get your boots."

He undid her boots, then his own. They were kicked to the side of the room. Next he pulled down her ski pants, leaving her with only a pair of wool socks and a pair of underpants. His ski pants came off, and she glanced at the bulge in his jockey shorts. As she did, he groped for his wallet in his pants.

The moment she saw the foil packets, she understood. The man came prepared. Even out of control, he was in control. She knew she should be thankful, but it irritated her. "Sure you didn't have this planned?"

Randall glanced at her, then at the foil packets he'd laid on the nightstand. "They've been there a long time. A very long time."

So long, he hoped they were still good. "I'm—" He paused. He was painfully hard and that worried him. "It's been a long time since I was with a woman."

"That so?"

She surprised him by touching him, the warmth of her hand sending shock waves through his body. He wrapped his hand around hers, stopping her. "You do that and I won't last long enough to get started."

"You mean there's something you can't control?" she said, an impish gleam in her eyes.

"Not if you keep that up."

She drew her hand away, and he sighed in relief. But the moment he sat on the bed, she was sitting on top of him, her legs straddling his thighs and the most feminine part of her pressing against his arousal. "Gina," he gasped, feeling himself grow even harder.

"Yes, Randall?" she asked innocently, all the while moving her hips so she was rubbing across him.

"Damn you." He couldn't stop himself. She was driving him crazy.

He rolled her off his lap, so she was lying on her back on the bed, then he rolled on top of her, switching their positions so he was straddling her, his knees on either side of her thighs. With one hand, he reached down and pulled off her panties. She wiggled beneath him, helping rather than stopping him. And then she pulled at his jockey shorts, and he felt them slip down on his thighs.

The shorts went and they were both naked except for their wool socks, and he didn't care about socks. Spreading her knees with his, he positioned himself over her. A caress told him she was ready. He started to reach for the foil packet on the nightstand but she also moved. Arching her back, Gina rubbed her hips against his.

Perhaps she only meant to tease him, as he'd teased her, and perhaps he should have had better control, but the motion was enough to bring them together, and he forgot the foil packet. One thrust, and hard entered soft, the pleasure coursing through him taking his breath away yet again.

Her eyes were wide and now the deepest of blues, and he knew he was lost, that he'd never had control, had had only the illusion. Protection forgotten, he thrust himself deep into her, enveloping himself in a heavenly glove of moist warmth. The groan he gave came from deep within, a sound of submission and satisfaction. Everything was forgotten. Everything except how wonderful she felt and how much pleasure she was giving and how nothing had ever been this good.

Gina knew she was being foolish, that she was taking a chance, but she'd wanted him this way, totally naked and out of control. She wanted him to be a part of her. No barriers. She wanted the physical to become spiritual, a blending of souls.

For her, the act of their bonding was more than sex. It was a bringing together of separate parts that didn't blend but enhanced. He brought out the best in her, made her feel. He made her body sing and the blood pound in her head.

His thrusts were wild, each carrying her higher to a pinnacle of pleasure she'd never known. In his savagery, he was her warrior, taming her needs as he tamed his own. He awoke sensations, excited them and made her want to cry out. She gripped his arms, her body tensed and her breath caught in her lungs.

Again and again, he thrust deep, drew back, then pressed into her again. She knew she was near, that her ecstasy was only a hairbreadth away, yet the moment it happened, the spasms shaking through her, she gave a gasp of surprise. He groaned and sank deep into her, fulfilling her pleasure as he found his own.

Only when her breathing returned to normal, did she realize what she had done.

10

Randall rolled to his back and stared at the ceiling. Myriad emotions surged through him, ranging from exhilaration to anger. He wanted to shout for joy, and he wanted to pound his head against a wall. He'd given in to his desires, and it had been wonderful. He'd done everything he'd promised himself he wouldn't do, and it had been better than he'd ever dreamed.

Gina stirred beside him, and he turned toward her, guilt tearing at his pleasure. He reached for her hand and gave her fingers a squeeze. "You all right?"

She looked as dazed as he felt. "I think so."

An apology seemed appropriate, something to ease his remorse. He came up with the best he could do. "That wasn't very smart on my part."

The moment he uttered the words, he felt her stiffen beside him and knew she didn't understand. Quickly he tried to explain. "I mean, not using any protection. I just—"

"Lost control?" she asked softly.

How easily she summed it up. Worse, she seemed pleased that he had.

"It should be okay," she said, but he noted a moment of hesitation.

"Okay?" He didn't see how anything could be okay, not after what they'd shared.

"I think it was safe. That is, it was safe as long as you don't have any diseases."

"No, no diseases." Unless you could classify a base nature as a disease.

"None here, either."

She was reassuring him, but he didn't feel he deserved her consideration. He was the one at fault. He'd practically forced her to come along on this car chase, had put her in this situation. It wasn't her fault he found her desirable or that he couldn't control himself.

Even now she was tempting him.

He arched up on one elbow and reached over to run a hand through her already mussed hair. Like spun taffy, the golden tresses fanned out around her face. They twisted into a tangled mess that defied his combing, and he switched to tracing an imaginary line down the side of her face. Her makeup was nonexistent, her lips swollen from his kisses, and her cheeks flushed. She looked like a woman who'd just made love.

She looked beautiful.

He leaned close, wanting another taste of her mouth, then felt her shiver. Again guilt assailed him, and he drew back. Even with the heater running, the room wasn't warm. Certainly not warm enough to be lying around wearing only a pair of socks.

"I'm cold," Gina said and wiggled away from him. "I don't know about you, but I'm getting under the covers."

In seconds, she was under the covers, sitting so she was leaning against the headboard, one of the two pillows propped behind her back and the blanket and chenille spread up to her chin. She smiled and patted the space beside her. "Join me?"

"I—" He stared at the spot she'd patted, then at the outline of her legs and hips. Suddenly he jerked his gaze away. He couldn't do this, he told himself. Shouldn't. Not again.

It was time to take control of his emotions. Earlier he'd had a need, but that need had been satisfied. He'd wondered what it would be like to make love with her, and now he knew. Now he could get on with his life.

Randall stood and looked around for his clothes. His pants lay on the floor next to Gina's, one leg halfway over the legs of hers. Even their clothing seemed to be making love.

He picked up his pair, then glanced her way.

Gina said nothing, disappointment tearing through her. She tried not to look down at his hips, yet her gaze was drawn that direction to the part of him that only a short while before had given her such pleasure. Now he was sated; the moment was over. *Slam, bam, thank you, ma'am.* If they weren't trapped by a snowstorm, he would be on his way. She knew the routine.

He stood there, staring at her, his pants dangling from his right hand. She looked back up at his face. He could stare all he wanted but he wouldn't know how she felt. She'd given of herself, and just as her body had been without protection, so was her heart. Long before today, he'd infiltrated that, but she wasn't going to ask him to stay.

To her surprise, Randall dropped the pants on the floor. She said nothing as he slipped into the bed beside her. This time she didn't worry that the sag of the mattress brought their hips together but she knew all was not right. He might be in bed with her, without a stitch of clothing on except for his socks, but he wasn't truly with her. Randall the businessman was beside her, reserved and proper.

"I think we need to talk," he said.

Even his tone was controlled, and that irked her. "About what?"

"About us."

"Is there an us?"

His hesitation was her answer. Biting her lower lip, she stared at the darkened television screen across the room. In it, she could see Randall's reflection. His hair was tousled and he looked ridiculous with a bedspread under his chin. He started to say something, then closed his mouth. She waited, wanting words of love, but knowing they wouldn't come.

"I like you," he finally said.

She continued looking at the television. "How nice."

"Gina?"

She couldn't answer, for to do so would reveal the pain. Tears stung her eyes, and she blinked them back.

"Gina, look at me."

Slowly she did, knowing the telltale moisture was there. He wiped away a tear with the tip of his finger, then huffed. "Damn you."

"Damn me?"

"Yes."

Of course, she should have known he would blame her. How like a man. She was about to tell him where he could jump when he swore again.

"Damn! Damn! Damn!"

Each word became softer and more endearing, the look in his eyes changing to desire. For a moment she was confused, then he reached for her, catching her by the shoulders and drawing her close. "Don't you realize what you're doing to me?" he asked.

"I'm not doing anything," she responded softly. At least, she didn't think she was. "I didn't want this to happen, Randall. Not really. Oh yes, I've thought about it, wondered what it would be like, but I know we're not right for each other, I know I'm just getting myself into another hopeless situation, and that I—"

"Hush." He touched a finger to her lips, the anger completely gone from his expression and the tenderest of smiles crossing his face. "You're right. It's not your fault. I shouldn't blame you for being irresistible. It's not your fault that I can't stop thinking about you, or that I want to make love with you again."

She heard the anguish in that confession and knew he wasn't going to walk away, not yet. Later he would remember his resolve and have regrets, but for the moment there was hope. Laying a hand on top of his, she gave her response. "Then what are you waiting for?"

He hesitated, then chuckled and nodded. "You're right. What am I waiting for."

He combed his fingers into her hair, then slipped his hand around to the back of her head, bringing her face closer to his, and she knew he was going to kiss her. Surprised that she could feel giddy all over again, she smiled.

"What?" he murmured near her mouth.

"This is better than anything I ever imagined," she confessed. "You're better."

"So are you," he responded. "So are you."

His kiss was warm and familiar, and she welcomed it. He wasn't promising a forever after or saying he loved her, but he wanted her, and for the moment that was enough. It had to be.

They kissed and they touched, discovered and excited. It was new yet familiar, each step slower this time, giving them a chance to fully participate and enjoy. When he slid a hand between her legs, his fingertips massaging her, she knew once had not been enough for her, either.

"It won't be as rushed this time," he promised. "This time it will be better for you."

He didn't understand how she'd reveled in his earlier lack of control, how for a time they'd been equal, each unable to stop the wanting. It might only be lust, but in those few minutes he'd given her a part of himself. She wondered how anything could be better.

Together they slipped farther under the covers so their bodies were flat on the bed, their hips touching. He played his fingertips between her thighs, teasing her with his touch and causing her to groan. She spread her legs, and he continued his stroking, all the while playing kisses over her mouth and face.

Within Gina a battle waged, the pleasure of prolonged tension warring with a desire for release. She wanted the foreplay to stop, yet she never wanted him to stop. Her body begged for relief, but drew pleasure from every stroke of his fingers. Holding her breath, she waited, then groaned when he moved his hand away.

She'd been so close. So very close.

He shifted position, leveling himself over her. Staring up at his face, Gina saw his smile. He knew how he was taunting her, that he was driving her wild. He knew how much she wanted him right now, that she was at his mercy, willing to beg for relief from this exquisite torture. Once again, he was in control.

"Good," he murmured, then touched her again, but this time not with his finger.

He rubbed his hips against hers, and she automatically arched her back, bringing their bodies into alignment. What had been soft was now hard, and he stroked her with his arousal, rubbing over and slipping into her, then out again. She was wet and warm, and going insane. She held onto his arms, her fingers digging into his flesh. She couldn't breathe and she couldn't think. She wanted him inside of her. Deep inside. And she wanted him to keep doing what he was doing, wanted the pleasure that mingled with the anticipation.

Gina groaned out his name. Once again, she was so close, so very close.

The climax came like a volcanic eruption, the tremors explosive and consuming. Then came the heat. Pouring through her, it swept her to a height she'd never before imagined.

He held her there, at the peak, held her in a blend of physical and emotional pleasure. She'd gone beyond the beyond to soar on a euphoric cloud. Eyes closed, she drifted, totally at peace.

Only slowly did she come back to reality.

A lazy relaxation began to seep through her, a lethargic sense of satisfaction. Making love, she knew, would never be the same.

Then she felt him move within her.

His body became tense, and she knew their needs had been transferred. He was now the taker, the one seeking pleasure. He became the beast, savage and wild, and control was forgotten. His pumping drove him deep, and she clung to his shoulders, certain she could take no more. Except she could. Each rhythmic stroke of his body produced a response. Satisfaction changed to need. Once again, she was clinging to him, holding her breath and on the edge.

"Oh yes," he groaned when she arched into him. "Oh yes."

He was hot and sweaty and lost in an act as primitive as mankind. His wild, pounding thrusts were frenzied and fierce. He took, and she received.

The bed creaked, the headboard banged against the wall,

but she didn't notice. Didn't care. She was with him, again caught in a journey with only one end in sight.

She knew he'd reached his climax when he groaned, the sound a sigh of final release. The thrusting of his hips came to a stop, the motion replaced by another, this one more subtle and gentle. The pulsating rhythm pushed from within. She followed his lead, her own pleasure washing over her, cleansing away all tension and bringing back the euphoria. Only this time the end was more rewarding, the journey more satisfying. This time he'd been with her, in her, and a part of her. They were opposites, and yet they were alike, two extremes creating one moment of magic.

Totally drained, she closed her eyes.

A pounding on the door woke Randall. In a haze, he called out. "What?"

"It is late," a woman's voice answered from the other side of the door. "If you want me to clean the room, I need to do it now."

Randall looked at the clock by the TV. It showed the time as just a little after two o'clock. For a moment, he couldn't remember if it was day or night or even what day it was, then it all came back—the snowstorm, the morning and making love with Gina.

"Just a minute," he yelled back at the maid and rolled toward Gina.

Her eyes were heavy with sleep but open, and she smiled, then stretched. "I guess that means we've got to get up."

"We could tell her to forget it." With Gina beside him, the scent of her so sweetly captivating and her mouth so tempting, he wasn't sure he wanted to get up. It had been a long time since he'd made love twice in an afternoon, but it had been a long time since he'd done a lot of the things he was doing with Gina. Maybe too long a time.

"I don't know about you," Gina said, pushing herself up to a sitting position, "but I'm hungry."

Seeing her sitting there, naked to the waist, created a hunger in him. It was low and intense. He wasn't sure when he'd turned into a sex maniac, but Gina seemed to be the catalyst.

"One of Hazel's hamburgers sounds good," she said and swung her legs out from under the covers. For a moment she hesitated, wrapping her arms around herself. "Brrr, it's cold."

"Then come back under the covers." He would be glad to keep her warm.

To his dismay, she shook her head and made a dash for the bathroom. He might have been truly disappointed if he hadn't heard her toss him a promise before closing the door. "We can check out that bed again after a hamburger."

He could live with that, he decided, and got out of bed himself. "Five minutes," he yelled through the outside door, not sure if the maid was still there or not. "We'll be out in five minutes."

"I'll be back," she responded.

Randall was dressed by the time Gina came out of the bathroom. In a way he was sorry he was when he saw she was still naked. But she hurried for her clothes, and he reminded himself that he could wait until after they'd eaten lunch.

It was snowing when they walked over to Hazel's Café, and the path that had been cleared earlier was already clogged in places. Once they entered the café, Randall realized he actually was hungry for more than sex. The smells from the kitchen stimulated his taste buds, and he glanced at the homemade pies displayed in a refrigerated case. The

weeks without her to talk to made me realize I wanted more than advice from her.''

Grace continued as if the story had been scripted. ''We were married three weeks after I got back from my cruise, and two days before my seventy-first birthday.''

''And she's still giving me more than advice,'' Don said with a grin.

''Hush,'' Grace admonished, and her cheeks turned red.

Randall stared at the couple. They were talking and acting like a pair of young newlyweds, yet he was looking at wrinkles and age spots. None of it made sense to him.

''Randall's grandmother is doing something similar,'' Gina said, drawing him out of his confusion.

''Not similar,'' he argued automatically.

She didn't stop. ''Ella's eloping with a man she used to be in love with over fifty years ago. They only recently made contact, and after all those years, the sparks were still there.''

''Sparks don't go away with time,'' Don said.

''They just become embers,'' Ralph joked, then both men looked at Leo, and Ralph added, ''for some.''

Carlie took Leo's hand in hers and lifted it to her lips, her gaze on his face. ''Embers can be fanned,'' she said coyly.

''Ooh, topic's getting hot.'' Ralph fanned his fingers.

''But you're saying age doesn't make any difference when it comes to falling in love or wanting to make love?'' Gina asked. The question sounded perfectly innocent but Randall knew exactly what she was getting at. She was still set on convincing him that what his grandmother was doing was fine and dandy.

Well, it wasn't fine and dandy, no more than making

love with Gina had been wise. He should have his head examined.

Edith answered Gina. "Age does make a difference," she said. "I think the older you are, the more particular you become. And sex isn't as important." She nodded at her husband and the others at the table. "These men make it sound like they're a bunch of Don Juans, but age does take its toll. Yet you're never too old to enjoy a loving touch."

"The desire's always there," Ralph added.

"You're just not always up to it," Don said.

"Or able to get it up," Ralph added, laughing.

"You men," Grace grumbled, then looked at Randall. "You must be very happy for your grandmother."

Randall grunted, unwilling to share his opinion regarding his grandmother's foolishness, but he did voice his concerns. "Don't you worry about being taken in?" he asked, looking directly at Leo.

The quick glance Leo gave Carlie said he understood. Leo's answer, however, was firm. "You can only be taken in if you don't know what you're getting into."

"And do you think a person in her seventies knows what she's getting into?" Gina asked.

The answers were immediate and about what Randall expected considering their ages. "Of course," Ralph said. "Know better than some of you younger people."

"Sorry," another voice interrupted. "Didn't see you two come in."

Randall glanced up to find Lilly standing just behind him. The waitress looked tired and a little frazzled. She pushed a lock of red hair off her forehead and handed him a menu.

"Coffee for the two of you?" she asked.

"Please." He looked over the menu, but his thoughts were on Gina. She was determined to prove her point. Stubbornly determined.

He found the trait irritating and fascinating. And more and more, he found the woman and her romantic notions harder to resist.

11

Randall and Gina ate while Ralph's group played cards. Because there were six of them, one couple sat out each game. The card playing was intense but the conversations and laughter never stopped. Bantering seemed as important as winning a hand of euchre, and as soon as Lilly cleared away Randall's and Gina's plates, Ralph asked them if they would like to stay and make up another foursome.

Gina hesitated, glancing at Randall. She'd been the one who had insisted on a hamburger, who'd promised they would return to the room after eating. With her hunger now sated, an afternoon of making love with Randall seemed a lot more appealing than playing cards.

But Randall's attitude had changed from when they'd been in the room. She knew exactly when it had occurred. The moment they began talking about his grandmother the walls had gone up, and for the last ten minutes Randall had been talking to Don about computers and completely ignoring her. At Ralph's suggestion they join the game, Randall didn't even look her way but simply said, "Sure. Why not?"

Suppressing her disappointment, Gina decided it wouldn't be a bad idea, after all. He liked these people, enjoyed the way they got along. Perhaps, she hoped, even though he was fighting the idea, Randall would see that growing old didn't mean a person stopped living. Perhaps he would better understand why his grandmother had taken off with Jack.

It was after dark when the card games broke up. Lilly was sitting at one of the booths, her feet propped up on the seat. She looked tired, and during the afternoon Gina had learned that the staff at Hazel's Café was as snowbound as the rest of them. All three—Lilly, Hazel and the cook—had spent last night in the café. At Gina's urging, the men—Randall included—had left extra big tips.

"It's stopped snowing," Carlie said the moment they stepped outdoors.

"Look." Don pointed toward the sky. "I see stars."

Gina looked and saw a scattering of twinkling lights where the clouds had parted, then she shivered as a cold wind cut through her. She was surprised when Randall slipped an arm around her shoulders and drew her close to his body, giving her some warmth and shelter. The gesture could be viewed as loving but Gina knew better than that.

Randall's attitude had remained distant all afternoon and into the evening. Oh, he'd been friendly enough at the table, but the intimacy wasn't there. Any hopes she might have had that their making love had changed their relationship were now gone.

Gina told herself she could accept that. After all, he'd never promised anything more than a roll in the sack. He'd said he wanted her; he hadn't said he loved her. No, she was the one who'd let that foolish emotion slip into the relationship. She was the one who would cry the tears when this trip was over. Oh, how she wished they'd had separate rooms.

In front of the motel, the eight of them went their separate ways, each couple walking to a different door. Gina was glad none of the group had the rooms next to theirs. Not that she was worried that they would hear a squeaking bed or thumping on the wall tonight. No, the way Randall was acting, there wouldn't be a repeat of the afternoon's activities.

Having made love twice with Randall should have satisfied her curiosity and quelled her desire, but it hadn't. Even as she waited for him to unlock the door, she couldn't stop the quivering in her stomach. Not that she would ask him to make love with her. If she had to hang on to the edge of the bed again to keep from rolling toward the middle, she would do it. If he could keep his distance, so could she.

The door swung open, and Gina stepped inside their room and slipped off her new jacket. She walked over to the hangers, all the while searching for something to talk about now that she was alone with Randall. Ralph and the others seemed the safest topic, so she voiced her impression of them. "Didn't you find those three couples inspiring?"

"Inspiring?" he asked, his tone suspicious.

"Well, you know what I mean." Perhaps *inspiring* wasn't the right word. Her jacket hung up, Gina faced Randall. "They're old—at least five of them are—but they're so full of life. They are the perfect examples of love, marriage and how to make the best of any situation."

She thought it was obvious and expected him to agree. Instead, he shook his head, and she realized he hadn't moved from the doorway. His posture was stiff and guarded, and even before he opened his mouth she knew she wasn't going to like what he had to say.

"I wouldn't make a good husband."

"Husband?" He'd totally misunderstood her. "I didn't say anything about you making a good husband. I was talking about Ralph and the others."

Randall shook his head. "Let's not kid each other. I know what you're getting at." He glanced at the bed. "Look, Gina, just because we made love earlier doesn't mean I've changed my mind about getting into a relationship with you."

She knew that, but he didn't have to make what they'd shared sound like a disease. "Look, yourself," she snapped, angry with herself for falling for another man who wouldn't commit. "If you want to be paranoid, fine, but I really was talking about Ralph and Edith, Don and Grace, and Leo and Carlie. I don't know about you but I find them inspiring, and if and when I ever do find a man who wants more than a roll in the sack, I hope we are as happy with each other as those six seem to be."

She started toward Randall, then stopped. Getting closer wouldn't help. For a communications major, she was doing a rotten job of communicating with Randall. She hadn't even convinced him to give up his chase after his grandmother. Not that she wasn't willing to give that one more try. "The way those couples feel about each other isn't so different from how your grandmother feels about Jack. Don't you see? Getting old doesn't mean you lose your desire to love and be loved."

Again he shook his head, his eyes narrowing. "My grandmother is not like those people."

"Yes, she is. She's just like them. Maybe *you* don't want a relationship, but your grandmother's not afraid of getting into one. She's with Jack because she cares about him, because he's giving her something she needs."

"That's the way you see it."

"Yes, that's the way I see it." And he was being too blind to open his eyes to the truth. "We all need love. Even you, though you won't admit it."

"Ah." He lifted a finger and pointed at her. "This is about us, isn't it?"

"No!" She was beginning to wonder if you could communicate with a brick wall. "Believe me, you've made it perfectly clear that you're not interested in anything more than sex." And she was tired of arguing with him. "You want to take but you don't want to give. You like the pleasures but not the responsibilities. You're so afraid you're going to be hurt, you refuse to live. Well, let me tell you, I wouldn't marry you if you asked, so don't bother worrying about it."

"I'm not worrying about it."

"Oh yeah?" She scoffed. "I think you've been worrying about it all afternoon."

"I don't want you getting the wrong idea."

"Wrong idea? Just because you—we—" She stopped. Arguing wasn't going to get her anywhere. He saw people as predators; she saw them as companions. They shared a common language but not a common view of life.

"Forget it," she said and turned toward the television. She snapped it on, then sat on the end of the bed, staring at the screen, not him.

She felt his eyes boring into her and sensed his anger. Tension filled the room, then she heard the outside door open and close. Only when she was alone did she allow her shoulders to sag and her breath to escape. Only then did she admit to herself how much it hurt that he didn't care.

Aimlessly she flipped from station to station, not really noticing what was on. Anger mingled with pain, sinking deep into her belly until it lay there like a water-soaked knot. Over and over she asked herself why she kept doing this, kept falling for men who wouldn't commit. What macabre sense of pleasure forced her to want what she couldn't have?

Tom loved her. He'd said so. He wanted to marry her. He'd asked. He'd made a commitment. So why had she turned him down? "Why?" she asked aloud.

Why had she let herself fall in love with Randall Watson?

She had no answer to either question and neither did the announcer on the television. She snapped off the power and walked to the window. With a twist of the rod, she opened the blinds, wondering where Randall had gone, considering his car was buried under four feet of snow.

She saw him immediately, pawing at the snow that covered his car. He didn't have an ice scraper, and he was using his hands. Though he had on gloves, Gina knew it wouldn't take long for the cold to permeate the material and turn his hands to ice.

Looking around the room, she found a couple of possible tools. She grabbed her coat, gloves and knit hat, then the ice bucket and the plastic glasses provided by the motel. Once outside, she said nothing to Randall, simply went to work using one of the plastic glasses to scoop snow from the hood of the car.

She left the ice bucket sitting near the windshield, and moved to the opposite side of the car. The motel owner had used the snowblower to clear a path between each of the vehicles parked in the lot, but four feet of snow in twenty-four hours had buried most of the cars above the hood.

Randall watched Gina scoop snow from the hood. She hadn't said a word since coming out of the room, had simply set that ice bucket on the hood, then walked around to the other side and begun working. He glanced at the ice bucket. "Mind if I use that?" It would be more efficient than his hands, which were getting darn cold.

"Please do." She gave him a quick glance then went back to work.

"I never realized how much snow could fall in such a short time," he said, pulling off his right glove and blowing on his fingers. "Or how cold it could be."

"That's snow for you. Cold."

He caught the sarcasm. She didn't look at him, simply kept working, and he was surprised when she spoke again. "I remember the first time my parents brought me up to Tahoe," she said. "I think I was four. Maybe five. I couldn't wait to get out and 'Pay in da no.'" She mimicked baby talk. "While Mom and Dad were unpacking the car, I decided to jump right in."

Gina shook her hands and gave a mock shiver. "Cold. I'd never felt anything so cold. I started crying. Screaming, my mother says." She laughed. "I didn't want to 'Pay in da no' after that."

"But you did." He remembered she'd said she came up often.

"Oh yes." She paused in her scooping and looked at him. "Once they had me properly dressed, I found out how much fun it could be. Besides, my sister, Carrie, didn't hesitate going out into it, and I did everything Carrie did. We'd sled. Build forts. Throw snowballs." She tossed a handful of snow his way, but it fell apart before it reached his side.

"And skied, you said earlier."

"Definitely. Carrie was always better than I, but I do love skiing." As she got closer to the metal finish of his car, Gina switched to using her gloved hand to swipe off the snow. "I was wise enough to learn I couldn't follow Carrie in everything she did. She tackled the advanced slopes, and I stuck to the medium level."

"Ever broken a leg or anything?" That was his fear.

"Sprained an ankle one year. Really badly. Kept me off skis for that season, but I was back the next year. What about you, Randall? What do you do for fun?"

"I play handball and golf." He shrugged, still scooping away at the mass of snow that covered his car. Truth was, he hadn't been doing either of those activities lately. "I really don't have time for fun."

"Now that's too bad. You should always have time for fun."

"Maybe in your world."

Her eyebrows rose. "In my world?"

"Well, you know what I mean." Not that he was sure he knew what he meant. "I have the business. There's not much time for fun and play."

"All work and no play makes—"

She left it dangling. He filled in the blanks. "A lot of money."

"Ah, but can money buy you happiness?"

"Made my grandfather and grandmother happy, and a lack of it sure made my mother miserable."

"But now you're all worried about someone taking that money away from your grandmother. I guess you're right. My world is different from yours." She moved to the back of the car. "I grew up in a household where we had enough money to be comfortable, but not so much that we worried about someone cheating us out of it or forgot to have fun." She paused to look at him. "I have wonderful memories of trips to the snow with my family. Memories of laughter and being together."

Taking trips and being together meant arguing to him. There was the time he'd gone with his parents to Greater America and his mother had started yelling at his father. And the time one of her boyfriends agreed to take them on a picnic, and the day had ended in a lot of swearing because things hadn't gone the right way. Even his grandfather had argued with his mother whenever they got together.

But Randall knew he would remember this trip for a long time to come. Perhaps for a lifetime. He would remember making love with Gina, kissing her and feeling her body surrounding his. He would remember her laughter and energy and the way she made everything fun, from a trip to a store to clearing snow from a car.

He paused to look at her, and remembered back to a conversation he'd had with his grandmother. "She's a hard worker," his grandmother had said. "Doesn't ask what needs to be done, just pitches in and does it."

His grandmother's house had showed the results of Gina's energy. Windows had been washed, moldings cleaned and cobwebs swept away. He hadn't hired Gina for her cleaning services, though he'd told her there would be some light housework involved.

"She turns work into fun," his grandmother had said. "We get talking, laughing, and the dirt just disappears. She's a lot like me, when I was young."

Randall wondered what his grandmother had been like when she was young. Ella Flemming had always seemed old to him, but in reality she'd only been forty-one when he was born, just ten years older than he was now.

She seemed old now, but would he hold a different opinion when he was in his seventies? Could his grandmother arouse lustful thoughts in a man her age?

Get your mind off it, he told himself and went back to scooping snow. His grandmother's age and physical appeal weren't the problems, it was her vulnerability. Widows were susceptible to sweet-talking Romeos, could easily be charmed into thinking they were in love again. His grandmother didn't know what she was doing.

Randall wasn't sure he knew what *he* was doing.

Around Gina, he was as vulnerable as his grandmother. Gina messed up his control. She got him arguing, had him defensive and uncertain. Had him questioning his own life-style and values. And worse, she got him hot and bothered every time she came close.

He was glad the width of a car separated them. But how was he going to spend another night lying next to her, especially now that he knew what it was like making love with her? How could he deny that he wanted her?

I want sex, not a relationship, he told himself. It's lust, not love.

After all, what good was love? He'd loved his father, only to be deserted by the man and virtually ignored. Chasing the blonde of the month was more important to R. J. Watson than loving a son.

And he'd loved his mother, but he'd seen how her pursuit of love had caused her misery. She'd taught him that love was foolish.

Most of all, he'd loved his grandparents, but always with a touch of uncertainty. He'd heard his grandfather yell at his mother. Over and over, Carl Flemming had threatened to kick his one and only daughter out of the house. Except she'd shown him. She was the one who left. Left him and received his cold shoulder.

Love, Randall Watson had learned, was conditional. To get it, you had to comply.

It was his grandmother who had loved him without reserve. And now she was running off with another man, leaving him just as his father had. He knew it was foolish to view his grandmother's actions that way, but then, as he'd said, love was foolish.

He'd gone full circle and had no answers, except as he looked at Gina, he knew he wanted to be closer than a car's width, wanted to hold her again and fill her with his need.

Maybe it would only be for tonight but he wanted her sweetness, her laughter and even her arguments.

All the while they worked, cleaning the car bit by bit, Randall battled his internal war. Finally enough snow had been cleared from the car to allow them to open the doors. Once the roads were cleared, they could leave.

"Now all I hope is that it doesn't snow tonight," Gina said, an eye on the sky.

Randall also looked up. More stars showed than earlier, a slice of the moon giving off some light. The storm had passed.

When he looked back at Gina, he realized she was hugging herself and shivering. Ruefully she smiled. "Snow's cold," she repeated from their earlier conversation. "Do you mind opening the door to the room. I'm freezing."

"Of course." He'd forgotten he had the only key. Quickly he let her into the room, following her and closing the door behind them.

Her cheeks were red, as well as her nose, and she was huddled forward, her teeth chattering. "I was fine up until those last few minutes," she said and started pulling off her gloves.

He tossed his on the table and reached for hers, helping her with the second glove. Next he pulled down the zipper of her jacket. "Got to get you warm," he said, and slipped the jacket from her shoulders.

She said nothing, but helped him as he slid the jacket down her arms. He tossed it onto one of the two chairs in the room, then took her hands in his, his fingers not much warmer than hers. He brought her hands up near his mouth and began blowing on them and rubbing them briskly.

She continued shivering, her teeth chattering, and he moved his hands up her arms, rubbing his palms over her sweater to try to stimulate her circulation. "You shouldn't have let yourself get so cold," he chastised.

"It...just...sort of...hit," she said, her wide blue-gray eyes locked on his face.

"And here I thought you were the expert on snow."

"Not an...expert...on...anything."

He wondered about that, wondered if maybe she wasn't an expert at stealing hearts. He slid his arms around her shoulders, drawing her close. He could say he wanted to use his body heat to warm her or he could be honest and simply admit he wanted to hold her. He hugged her close, pulled her knit hat from her head and blew into her hair.

She resisted for a moment, remaining stiff in his embrace, then she melted against him, snuggling her cheek against his jacket and giving a sigh.

He continued rubbing his hands up and down the back of her sweater and began dropping kisses along the side of her face. Drawing her with him, he took two steps toward the window, reached over and twisted the blinds closed, then went back to caressing her and kissing her face.

He knew when her teeth stopped chattering, and he knew when she felt the change in his body. She tilted her head up slightly, a question in her eyes. Gently he kissed her on the lips, her mouth still cold but her response warm. Then he drew back and smiled down at her.

"I know a way to get you warm. In fact, it will warm us both up."

She glanced at the bed the same time he did, then back at him. "It might work."

"We should at least give it a try."

One more time, he told himself. Just this night. Not because he loved her but because he needed her and she needed him. It had nothing to do with love. Nothing at all.

He kept telling himself that as he slowly removed her

clothing, then his. Yet as he slipped under the covers beside her, then drew her close, feeling her give a shiver and wanting to chase it away, he wondered what emotion it was that was warming him clear to the core of his being.

12

—◆—

Gina woke to the sound of a car's engine running outside the room and a man calling to someone. She couldn't make out the words but she sensed it was a goodbye. People were leaving the motel.

She knew she was alone in the bed, but the voice outside her door hadn't sounded like Randall's. She sat up and listened to see if she heard him in the bathroom.

No sounds reached her ears from that room.

Once again he'd left, and she would bet he hadn't left a note saying where he'd gone. But she had a feeling she knew where he was. His need for coffee in the morning seemed to be as great as hers. At least they had that in common.

To be honest, she realized, they had a lot in common. Yesterday afternoon in Hazel's Café, she'd heard Randall's views on politics and the economy. He'd shared them with Ralph and the others while playing cards, and for once she hadn't argued with him. In fact, she'd often agreed.

She'd also discovered that he wasn't as callous as he sometimes sounded. But then, she'd known that Randall was a caring and giving man. She'd seen that demonstrated in the way he treated Ella, and Ella had told her of things Randall had done for his employees, things that went beyond the requirements of being a boss. Randall was honest and hardworking, a man who cared about others. He was exactly what she was looking for in a husband, except for one little flaw.

He didn't want a relationship.

"You did it again, Gina Leigh," she said aloud, then laughed at her foolishness. Over the past two days she'd been analyzing Randall and his behavior. Maybe it was time to analyze her own behavior. There had to be a reason why she was drawn to men who wouldn't commit.

Her parents certainly weren't the reason. She couldn't fault their relationship. With each other and with their children, they were loving, fair and compassionate. If anything, she wanted exactly what they had.

So had her sister. Carrie had said as much. And when Carrie married Vince, it seemed she'd found that relationship. "Except it didn't work."

Saying it aloud helped Gina make the connection. She'd always looked to Carrie as her role model. Carrie's romance with Vince had been Gina's idea of perfection. Carrie got married right after high school, had a beautiful wedding, and within two years had two beautiful babies. And then the perfect picture went bad.

And Gina began dating men who wouldn't commit.

It was a way to keep the perfect picture from going bad, she realized, and in a twisted way it made sense. It also helped explain why once a relationship broke up, she didn't feel more pain or shed more than a tear or two. Whenever a man said goodbye, she simply licked her wounds and went on. After all, why should she weep and wail? She'd gotten exactly what she wanted.

Except this time wasn't like the other times. This time, Gina knew, she was going to feel pain and it would be more than a tear or two she shed. Her feelings for Randall went deeper. It wasn't pretend. This time she'd truly fallen in love.

And she couldn't believe Randall didn't share that feeling. Last night he'd been so loving. He'd warmed her body with his caresses and kisses, and when she continued to shiver, he'd taken her by surprise, touching his lips to the essence of her womanhood and teasing her to a fevered pitch with his tongue. The fire he'd ignited had burned through her body until she'd cried out his name, begging him to take her. Willingly he'd obliged, burying himself deep within her. He'd used protection, but he couldn't protect her from the memories she would carry for a lifetime. He would always be a part of her, no matter if she never saw him again. When he said goodbye, the tears would be there.

Randall stood in line at the café, waiting to pay for two coffees. Four people were ahead of him, the two at the register arguing with Hazel about their bill. The couple had been bickering since he'd come in, the looks they shared almost hateful. Randall hadn't seen either before and assumed from what he overheard, that they'd come down from the lake early that morning. Their conversation reminded him of the arguments between his father and mother when he was young.

"Now, there's a divorce waiting to happen," Ralph said in a hushed voice behind him, and Randall turned slightly to find the older man also standing in line.

"Exactly why I have no intention of ever getting married."

"Oh yeah?" Ralph cocked an eyebrow, then nodded toward a young couple an unfamiliar waitress was leading to a table. "What about love? What about couples like that?"

Randall nodded back toward the bickering couple, the

man still arguing with Hazel about the bill. "They were probably like that once."

"Maybe," Ralph said. "Or maybe not."

Randall laughed. "Oh, that's a great answer."

"Love's a crap shoot."

"I don't like to gamble."

"Sometimes you just gotta take a chance."

"Yeah, right." Randall had heard that before, usually from his mother. She'd taken several chances and had been burned just as many times. Well, maybe not this last time, but that was yet to be seen.

The outside door opened and another man came in, another one Randall hadn't seen before. His face was flushed with the cold and he was wiping his gloved hands on his ski jacket and breathing hard. He came directly toward Ralph and Randall, looking at the two foam cups in Randall's hands. "How do I get a couple of coffees to go?"

"Ask her." He nodded toward the waitress who was working behind the counter. "She'll get them for you."

"Thanks," the man said and stepped that way.

"You just come down from the lake?" Ralph called after him.

The man paused and looked back their way. "Yeah. Just stopped here to take off my chains and get some coffee."

"You needed chains coming down?" Randall had thought with the storm over the roads would be clear.

"From the lake down to Kyburz it's R2 conditions. If you have a four-wheel drive, they'll let you on the highway without them, otherwise you have to have them on."

"Damn." Randall grumbled his disappointment. It might have stopped snowing, but he was no better off than before. Then he thought of something and looked back at the man. "You just took your chains off? What kind of car do you have?"

* * *

Gina was drying her hair when Randall came into the room. He was carrying two foam cups and she could smell the coffee. "Wonderful," she said, walking toward him.

"More than wonderful," he said, grinning. "Guess what else I bought this morning?"

She cocked her head. She could see his hands and he wasn't carrying anything but the cups. He could have stuffed something in his back pocket, but she had no idea what. "I give," she said, trying to peek around to see his backside.

"Chains."

"Chains?"

He continued grinning. "One set of slightly used chains that cost me an arm and a leg. I must have sounded desperate. You could almost see the dollar signs in the guy's eyes when he looked at me."

"You bought another driver's chains?" It took a moment for the idea to sink in. "From someone we know?"

"No, this was some guy on his way down from the lake. He said the roads are good. Slow, but good. Oh, and Hazel said to tell you that Lilly finally got home, and she really appreciated what you did for her."

"What did I do for her?" Gina couldn't remember doing anything but talking to the waitress.

Randall grinned again. "You talked all of us into leaving the woman a substantial tip, certainly far more than I normally would have left. Now..." He looked around the room. "I think we'd better hit the road as soon as possible. There might still be a chance we can stop my grandmother."

He hadn't changed his mind, and that disappointed Gina. She'd hoped the time they'd spent with Ralph and the others would open Randall's eyes to his grandmother's needs. A false hope, she now realized.

"I'm going to try calling her," Randall said. "Then I'll get those chains on. You want any breakfast?"

"No." She couldn't eat, not now. The old Randall Watson was back: efficient, determined and single-minded. He would stop his grandmother from marrying Jack, no matter what. And if he couldn't stop her—?

Gina wasn't sure what he would do, but she knew he wouldn't simply walk away. The only thing he would walk away from was love.

She gathered her clothes together and put them in the car while Randall tried the numbers for the two Longmans listed in Lake Tahoe. The phones were still out, giving him no answer, so he put the chains on the car while Gina stayed in the room and watched the morning news. Once the motel bill was paid and Randall's things were in the car, they hit the road.

They said very little to each other, but Gina could read his body language. The wall was back up between them. Last night their bodies had been united, but this morning they were two separate entities. She wanted to say something, but nothing she'd learned in college had taught her how to argue unemotionally when your heart was involved. It was easier to avoid a confrontation by remaining silent. So she said nothing.

At the checkpoint for chains, they were waved through, and Gina forced herself to concentrate on the scenery. The cedars and pines were heavy with snow and the landscape looked like a snapshot from a Christmas card. Steep drop-offs edged the highway and she was glad for the extra traction the chains provided. Though the snowplows had been through, they'd merely scooped off the top layers and packed down the rest.

As soon as they neared the lake, the tranquil scenery changed. From Meyers on, their surroundings became more commercial. More and more motels and restaurants lined the highway as they approached the state line, and once they drove over the boundary, the casinos and hotels took over. Fancy marquees announced the presence of big-name stars, and people were already gambling. Perhaps not as many as there would be that evening, but Gina could see them just inside the doorways, playing the slot machines. Over and over, men and women of all sizes and shapes dropped in their coins, pumping the levers that gave the slots the nickname of "one-armed bandits."

She saw Randall frown when they passed a wedding chapel. Without a break they drove on, through Kingsbury and Round Hill Village to Zephyr Cove. The nearer they got to the area, the more landmarks Gina recognized from comments Jack had made in his letters. "I think it's somewhere around here," she said, noting a store that had a closed sign on the door. "I remember him writing that he and his wife used to walk from their place to the little store on the highway. He said it was exactly one mile round trip."

"So the house is within a half-mile radius?" Randall looked around.

"If that's the right store." She had no way of knowing. No more than she knew which road Jack and his wife would have taken. Several cut off from the main highway.

"Right or left?" Randall asked, slowing as he neared one road that went either direction.

"Left," Gina said. "I know the house is near the lake."

What she didn't know was how close to the lake. Several were built almost on the shoreline; others sat back farther, nestled among the trees. None of the houses they drove past showed any signs of life, no footprints or tire tracks. Gina kept trying to remember the pictures Jack had sent and what he'd written. So much had been general information. He'd talked about the chipmunks he regularly fed and the Steller's jays that rudely yelled at him whenever he stepped outside, demanding the pine nuts they knew he would provide. He'd mentioned how the snow stayed on the mountaintops even in July, and how he could see it from his living room window.

Whenever they passed a clearing among the trees she could see the mountaintops Jack had been talking about. They were completely covered with snow now, as was everything around them. "I don't know," she said, looking back at Randall. "I have no idea which house it might be, or if this is even the right road."

"Then I guess we ask for help." Randall pointed down the road.

Bundled in warm clothing, a figure was shoveling the snow away from the driveway in front of a house. Randall drove up beside the figure and rolled down the window. "Excuse me," he called out. "We're looking for someone."

The bundled figure stopped shoveling, straightened and looked their way, and Gina saw it was a man. Probably in his sixties, his face was red from the cold and a cloud of cold air escaped from his mouth when he answered. "Who you looking for?"

"A Jack Longman. We believe he lives around here, but we don't know for sure."

"Jack Longman." The man smiled and leaned his shovel against a fence post before stepping closer to Randall's car. "Sure, I know him. Knew his wife, too." He shook his head sadly. "Shame her going like that. I hear she really suffered toward the end. She used to be so healthy looking."

Randall tried to get the man back on track. "Can you tell us which house Jack lives in?"

If he could, he wasn't going to, at least not yet. The shoveler leaned down and smiled at Gina. "You two related to Jack?"

"No," Randall said quickly. At least, he hoped he wasn't.

"They had a couple kids." The shoveler straightened and went on. "A girl and a boy. Of course, they're grown and married now. Have children of their own." He frowned. "I think Jack said he had five grandchildren now." He shook his head. "Not sure about that."

"Do you know the address?" Randall prompted.

The shoveler frowned. "Any particular reason you're looking for Jack? I mean, he's not in any trouble, is he?"

"No, no trouble." Unless Jack was trying to dupe his grandmother, Randall thought. "He's up here with my grandmother, and we're…" He paused, deciding it would be best to couch what he said. "We're supposed to meet them but we lost the address."

"Ah." The shoveler nodded knowingly. "I thought I saw his car go by a couple days ago. Can't really miss that yellow Cadillac. I would have called him, but the phones have been out." He shook his head. "You'd think they'd be able to keep the phones working. On the TV, they said it was something in the main office that went bad. No telling when they'll have them working again. Sure hope no one had an emergency during this storm. Couldn't call for help if they did. That's for sure."

"The address?" Randall persisted.

Again the shoveler frowned, as if he'd forgotten what they were talking about, then he nodded. "Not exactly sure what the number is." He pointed up the road. "You go about a quarter of a mile, then take the dirt road that heads down toward the water. Well, I guess you can't tell it's dirt because of all this snow, but it is. Jack's is the second house. You can't miss it. Looks like one of those Swiss chalets. Has green shutters with yellow and red flowers. Real pretty.''

"Thank you," Randall said with a sigh of relief and put his car into gear.

"You tell him Lou Simon says hi, okay?" the shoveler called as Randall rolled up his window and started in the direction the man had pointed.

"So you've found her."

The sound of Gina's voice surprised him. She'd been quiet all during his discussion with the shoveler. That in itself had been unusual. Now he heard a tone of defeat. He glanced her way. "Hopefully I have."

"And what are you going to do now? Drag her kicking and screaming from Jack's place? Am I to hold her down while we drive back? Keep her from killing you?"

He could imagine his grandmother reacting that way. There were times when she got upset that she let loose with her temper. This might be one of those times. But he didn't intend on that happening. "I'm going to talk to her."

"But are you going to listen to her?"

"Of course." He looked Gina's way again and saw her disbelief. That she thought he wouldn't listen hurt.

Well, maybe he didn't always listen. He hadn't listened when his grandmother told him about Jack. Two days had lessened the shock of discovering his grandmother had a boyfriend. Shoot, by now, she might have a husband.

"I will listen," he repeated.

"And?"

"And I don't know. I guess I'll see how she's acting. Check the guy out."

Gina decided that was better than the attitude he'd started with, though he still sounded more like a father checking on his daughter's welfare than a grandson checking on his grandmother. "He's a nice guy," Gina insisted, hoping she was right.

"We'll see."

When they found the road Lou Simon had described, they saw a quaint two-story house, built like a Swiss chalet, complete with the decorative trim and painted shutters. The house faced the lake, and a path to the front door was cleared of snow as well as the drive to the separate garage. As far as Gina could tell, no car had left the garage that morning. No tire tracks were evident on the side road except for the ones they were making. In fact, she was surprised the road had been plowed.

Randall parked the Lexus, but didn't immediately get out. For a moment he simply stared at the house, then he let out a breath. "Well, the place doesn't look too bad."

"Not too bad at all," she agreed.

"Can't be cheap living here on the lake."

"Probably not."

His look said he knew she was mocking him. "She's my grandmother," he said.

"She's a grown woman."

He grumbled and opened his door, and Gina knew he wasn't going to listen to Ella. Randall had made up his mind. Come hell or high water, he was going to rescue her from her folly.

Gina debated staying in the car and out of the battle, but it was already getting cold with the heater off. Reluctantly she opened her door and got out. Slowly she followed Randall up the walk to the front door.

She half prayed no one would answer Randall's knocks. She could have been wrong. A car might have left that morning. Maybe the wind had filled in the tracks. The wind was blowing.

Her hopes were dashed when the front door opened and

a lean, white-haired man with startling blue eyes faced them.

Jack Longman was shorter than Gina had imagined, probably not more than five foot nine. His face was lined with wrinkles, but there was a vigor about him that clearly stated he was not a dottering old man ready to spend the rest of his years in a rocking chair. He was wearing tan trousers, a polo shirt and a vest. Loafers covered his feet.

Randall, Gina noted, was carefully looking Jack over. Making his own assessment, she was sure. Just what his conclusions were, she didn't know.

"Can I help you?" Jack asked cautiously, glancing at both of them.

Randall's frown was enough reason to call for caution. His gruff response only added to her concern. "What have you done with my grandmother?"

13

———►◄———

"**A**hh." Jack Longman nodded in understanding, then turned to call back into the house. "Ella, your grandson is here."

He opened the door wider and stepped back, limping ever so slightly. "Come on in. We've been expecting you."

"Expecting us?" Randall looked around the interior of the house. The furnishings were attractive—nothing ornate or terribly expensive. A curved staircase ran from the foyer to the upstairs, and the railing was decorated with cutout designs similar to those on the outside of the house. To his left was the living room, complete with beige carpeting, a sofa covered in flowered chintz, two solid-colored armchairs, end tables and a coffee table. Bookshelves lined the walls next to a huge stone fireplace and framed pictures sat on the marble mantel. Comfortable and practical were words he would use to describe the decor.

"My neighbor down at Rossmoor called two days ago," Jack answered. "Just before the phones went out. He said his wife had talked to you. Said she had a feeling you were going to try to catch up with us."

"Did you get caught in the storm?"

Randall turned toward the staircase at the sound of his grandmother's voice. She came down the steps regally, wearing a red velvet lounging robe trimmed in gold. Her hair was indeed blond—champagne blond—and she looked ten years younger than the last time he'd seen her. She'd even put on lipstick, and her smile was welcoming, but he thought he caught a flicker of concern in her eyes.

"We had to spend two nights at Lascott," he said and walked toward her. "You're okay?"

"Fine. Absolutely fine." Her smile widened to a grin when she reached the bottom step, and she looked over to where Gina and Jack stood. "We made it up here before the worst of the storm hit. Those last few miles, you would have thought Jack was driving another Indy 500."

"Trying to relive my youth," Jack said, then went on to explain. "I spent nine years on the circuit. Never did win the Indy 500, though I came close a couple of times. I don't imagine you ever heard of me." He looked at Randall, then at Gina. They shook their heads, and Jack shrugged. "No, I didn't think you would have."

"He made his name and fortune after he retired from racing," Ella said, her look expressing her pride in his accomplishments. "He made modifications to the Indy cars. The ones he sold to racers were safer and faster."

He sold cars. Randall remembered Gina telling him that. He'd assumed she meant passenger cars.

He'd made a lot of assumptions lately. He'd assumed a man in his seventies, one who'd been injured in the war, would drive slow and be easy to overtake. Big mistake.

"You look good," Randall said to his grandmother.

Her attention came back to him, her smile motherly. "And so do you." She brushed a fingertip over his cheek, her blue eyes bright with energy. "You look more rested than I've seen you in a long time. Happier."

Her gaze switched to Gina. "And how are you, my dear?"

"Not too bad."

"Keeping my grandson in line?"

Gina gave a stilted laugh. "Hardly."

Randall could tell Gina was uneasy. She was probably waiting for him to erupt. Which he still might do. He frowned at his grandmother. "So what did you do, Grandma? Plan this whole thing to get Gina and me together?"

Ella's eyebrows went up as she looked back at him. "Now how was I to know you'd drag Gina along? Or that you'd even follow us? You shouldn't have, you know. With all the newscasts we've been hearing about this snowstorm and the people who were trapped by it, we've been quite concerned about you two."

"You certainly left enough clues to entice us to follow you," he accused.

"Me?"

"Yes, you. That message on my voice mail and the note you left for Gina. You had to know I'd bring her along. How else could I find you?"

Gina interrupted before Ella could answer. "If you told him where Jack lived, he didn't remember."

"Ah, as usual, you weren't listening to me, Randall," Ella winked at Gina. "Been a problem of his since he was a child."

"Whether I was listening or not is beside the point," Randall grumbled. "We were talking about your plot to get Gina and me together."

"Which wasn't a plot," Ella insisted. "The phone message and note were because Jack and I hadn't planned this. That's what made it so much fun. The idea of eloping has always sounded romantic to me. When I told Jack that, he said, 'Let's do it. Let's elope tomorrow.' So we did. Did what I should have done a long time ago."

Her gaze drifted to Jack, who was grinning and looking

at Ella with adoration. Gina knew then that the only thing Jack Longman wanted from Ella was the love she had to give. To stop them from getting married would be wrong.

"Have you really thought this over?" Randall asked, his tone concerned.

Ella looked back at him. "For more than fifty years. Oh, not every day, mind you, but the question was always there. 'How would my life have turned out if I'd disobeyed my parents and run off with Jack?'" She shook her head. "I'll never know the answer to that but I did know I wasn't going to spend the remainder of my years asking myself that question. So, Randall, if you've come to stop me from marrying Jack, I'm afraid you're too late. We are married. Have been for—"

She paused and looked at Jack. He glanced at his watch and answered for her. "Forty-five hours and fifteen minutes."

Ella stepped away from the staircase and walked over to Jack's side, slipping her arm through his. Visually united with Jack, she faced Randall again. "I am now Ella Longman."

Randall said nothing, simply blew out a long breath.

Gina was delighted with the news. "Congratulations," she said and shook Jack's hand. Then she gave Ella a hug. "May you enjoy many years of happiness."

"Amen to that," Jack said, gazing at his new bride. Then he looked at Randall. "I hope you realize I've loved your grandmother for a long, long time. Not that I didn't love my wife. Dora and I had a wonderful life together, had two wonderful children, who in turn have given us five wonderful grandchildren, but your grandmother always held a special place in my heart."

"As he held a special place in my heart," Ella said, leaning against Jack's arm and resting her head on his shoulder while looking at Randall. "I also loved your grandfather. I hope you can understand that."

For a moment, Gina didn't think Randall was going to answer. He stared at his grandmother and Jack in silence, his expression unreadable. Only after what seemed an eternity did he give a nod. "I'm beginning to understand a lot of things about love that I hadn't before." He paused, seemingly considering something, then went on, "By the way, I called and talked to Mother. She said to give you her best wishes."

Ella beamed. "I'd told her the last time we talked that I was hoping Jack would pop the question. Once these phones are working, I'll call her. She's been very supportive of my feelings."

"So I gathered," Randall said.

"And how is Hal?"

"Doing well right now, she said. She—" Randall stopped, his expression pensive, then he smiled. "She sounded happy."

"I do believe she is," Ella said, nodding again. "I think she has finally found the right man."

"After a lot of mistakes." Randall looked at Gina, and she knew what he was thinking. He wasn't going to make those mistakes.

"Life's a gamble," Ella said, and Randall jerked his head her way.

"That's the second time I've heard that today."

"It's the truth," Jack said. "Sometimes you've just got to take the chance. That's been my philosophy all my life."

"I was the one who wasn't willing to take a chance years ago," Ella said.

"Take a chance." Randall looked back at Gina, and she couldn't quite read his expression. When he started her way, he kept his gaze locked with hers. Only when he was a few feet from her did he stop. "Looks like I dragged you here for nothing."

"Looks like it." Though she was glad she'd had the opportunity to see Ella this happy. And she was glad Randall was accepting his grandmother's happiness.

"Gina's quite a woman," he said, glancing his grandmother's way. "But then, you knew that, didn't you?"

"I liked her right off," Ella said.

"She is stubborn, though, and she sure likes to argue. Flirts with everyone."

"I do not." Gina felt like an outsider listening in on a conversation. They were talking about her as if she wasn't even there.

"All right." Randall modified his earlier statement. *Talks* to everyone. And within minutes, they think she's wonderful."

"Because she is," Ella said, a warmth to her words.

He gave his grandmother a smile, then looked at Gina. "She does plays a mean hand of poker. Cheats, I think."

"I do not," Gina argued. "Would you like to explain what this is leading up to?" The intensity of Randall's gaze was making her nervous.

"I'm just listing your good points," he answered calmly before glancing his grandmother's way again. "She also throws a mean snowball."

"Skis well, I believe," Ella added. "You two should go skiing while you're up here."

Gina was sure Randall would tell his grandmother that they wouldn't be staying, that he had to get back to work. Instead he smiled. "So now you want her to give me skiing lessons? Hmm, that would mean we'd have to stay here for a while, would have to spend more time together. What do you think, Gina? Is she trying to get us together and keep us together?"

Gina looked at Ella. It did make sense. "Are you? Did you do this to get us together?"

Ella looked hurt by the question, then grinned. "Well, not completely. I did want to elope. And I knew Randall would try to stop me. I hoped you'd come along if I left that note but I didn't plan on that snowstorm. We were really worried about you two."

Being manipulated by Randall to come along had been irritating, but discovering that Ella had played on their weaknesses to get them together angered Gina. "How could you?"

Gina could tell Ella hadn't expected that response. The older woman's smile disappeared. "I just thought you two would be good for each other. You look so wonderful together."

As if that guaranteed happiness. "Nice-looking couples get divorces," Gina snapped. "If you don't believe me, ask my sister."

"We have very little in common," Randall added, supporting her argument. "She looks at the world through rose-colored glasses. Believes in love."

"And he doesn't," Gina said. He'd made that point often enough.

Randall smiled, then looked at his grandmother and Jack. "This is going to sound like a rather odd request, but could you two leave us alone for a while? Gina and I need to talk something out."

Ella studied him, frowning.

"Please?" he asked. "You conned us into coming up here together. Now that I know you're all right, Gina and I need to figure out what we're going to do next."

Ella lifted her eyebrows quizzically, then took Jack's hand. "Come on, dear," she said. "We need to make the bed."

"But we made the bed," Jack said.

"Then we'll unmake it." At the bottom of the staircase, Ella paused and looked at Gina. "Remember this, my dear. He has his faults but he is good-hearted."

"She makes me sound like a puppy dog," Randall grumbled and watched his grandmother and Jack disappear up the stairs. Then he looked back at Gina.

She shook her head. "You were right," she said. "I can't believe she really came here just to get us together."

"I wonder if she realizes just how much she got us together." Randall smiled, then laughed. "From what I've been hearing about these horny seventy-year-olds, she probably does." He glanced toward the living room. "Shall we go in there and sit down?"

He pointed toward the chintz-covered sofa that faced the pane glass window overlooking the lake. Gina decided sitting sounded like a good idea. All of these revelations were becoming too much for her. Or maybe it was too little sleep and too much lovemaking, but her legs were rubbery and sitting seemed far safer than depending on them to hold her up.

Randall, she noticed, kept a distance between them when they sat, and he shifted positions twice before he said anything. Even then, he didn't look at her. "Strange," he started, staring out the window, "I can talk in front of the board of directors without hesitation, and I make business decisions every day without having any trouble knowing what to say, but right now—" He looked at her. "Suddenly I'm tongue-tied."

"Why?" She didn't understand.

"Because I've never done this before." He blew out a breath, then gave a stilted laugh. "Well, I guess I did once. But that was a mistake." He reached over and took her left hand in his. "Okay, here goes. Gina, last night you told me I was only interested in sex. You said I only wanted to take, that I didn't want to give. That I liked the pleasures, but not the responsibilities.''

"I was angry," she said, surprised he'd remembered her words so well.

"With good reason," he admitted. "You also said I was so afraid of being hurt I refused to let myself take chances. Well, you were right, and I've been thinking about that. I guess we shouldn't be surprised or even angry that my grandmother did this to get us together. I certainly wasn't going to make the move on my own. It didn't matter that I was attracted to you, I wasn't going to take a chance on being hurt.''

Gina didn't know what to say. This was the most Randall had ever revealed to her about his thoughts.

He continued without stopping. "She probably knew I wouldn't be able to resist you if we were together very long. She probably figured I'd be foolish enough to think making love with you would help me get you out of my thoughts.''

Gina knew that had been his reasoning. Even she had initially participated in their lovemaking for exactly the same reason. She'd wanted to get him out of her system. Except for her, it hadn't worked out that way.

"I thought," he went on, "that if I could get through these years, when I was older I wouldn't care about sex. Then we go and talk to Ralph and the others—" He nodded toward the staircase. "And I hear my grandmother telling Jack they're going to unmake the bed." He shook his head. "I'm beginning to believe you never get too old for love.''

"You don't. People need love all of their lives.''

"You had a man in love with you," Randall said, almost accusingly. "That Tom guy. He wanted to marry you and you turned him down. Why?''

"Because I didn't love him. I told you that."

"And how do you know when you're in love?"

"You just know." She felt tears sting her eyes and looked away, blinking them back. "You don't see it coming. It just suddenly hits you. You try to fight it but you can't stop it."

She'd certainly tried fighting it. She didn't want to love Randall but she couldn't stop herself.

"Does it make you irritable?"

"Sometimes." She felt irritable now. On edge and uneasy. They were talking about love in the abstract but her feelings were real.

"Unsure of yourself?" he asked.

"Yes." She hadn't been certain of anything since meeting him.

He grunted a response, and she looked back at him. "So what's your point?"

"That sometimes I get the feeling my grandmother is smarter than I give her credit for. The question is, are you willing to change your mind?"

"About what?" She was completely confused.

"About marrying me."

"Marrying you?" She repeated the words, frowning as she did. This wasn't something she wanted to joke about.

"Yes. You said you wouldn't marry me if I asked but I'm asking anyway."

"Are you trying to be funny?" She stood, afraid to stay and let him see how much his proposal bothered her.

He also stood, rising next to her. "No. This is no joke. I'm asking you to marry me."

"You?" She pointed a finger at his chest and spoke slowly. "You want to marry me?" It was too fast a turn-around. He had to be kidding.

"Yes."

She closed her eyes, unable to stop the exhilaration surging through her even though she was sure there was a catch to what Randall was saying.

"I know I wouldn't make a perfect husband," he said. "I haven't had the best training. But I also know I wouldn't make my love conditional, not like my grandfather did. And I would never walk out on you or chase other women. I'm not like my father."

"Randall?" She opened her eyes slowly and looked up at him, still not sure this wasn't a game he was playing. A very cruel game. "You are really asking me to marry you?"

"Yes." He looked down at the carpeting. "I'll get down on my knees if that's what you want."

He started to kneel, but she stopped him. She didn't need him on his knees. She just needed to know he was serious, that he loved her. "Why?" she asked.

"Why? You have to ask why?"

Maybe she shouldn't. Maybe she should just be happy he'd asked. "I need to know," she answered. "I don't want you marrying me just because you heard a few men say you never outgrow the need for love. If I get married, I want it to last."

"I keep hearing that love's a gamble, that you don't know if it's going to last, that you just have to take a chance. I guess the question is, are you willing to take a chance on me?"

"No, the question is, do you *love* me?"

He smiled. "If it's not love, I don't know what you'd call it. What about you? Do you love me?"

She hesitated, afraid to reveal her feelings, then shrugged. "I tried not to."

"Same here. Didn't work for me."

She looked up into his eyes. "You are serious about this?"

He laughed and reached for her, catching her by the arms and bringing her close. "Very serious," he said, drawing her up on her toes. "Gina Leigh, like it or not, I've fallen in love with you. And if you don't agree to marry me, I may just have to kidnap you again and stow you in a motel room where I can keep you forever."

"Peter, Peter, Pumpkin eater," she began.

"Had a wife and couldn't keep her," Randall continued.

"So he kept her in a pumpkin shell," they said together, then laughed.

"I do love you," he said again, just before his lips touched hers.

He played his mouth over hers and she leaned into him, confused by everything that had happened but happier than she'd ever been. Then suddenly he drew back and looked down at her. "What about kids?" he asked.

She swallowed hard. They hadn't discussed children. It wasn't something you discussed with a man you weren't even going to have a relationship with after all. "Do you like kids?"

"I think so." He considered the idea, then grinned and brushed another kiss across her lips. "I think I'd like our children. I'd love a little girl who looked like you. I bet you were adorable as a child."

She shook her head. "Skinned knees and bruises all the time. I was a real tomboy."

Randall laughed "Wouldn't you know it. So will you marry me?"

She was beginning to believe him. "Say when and where, and I'll be there."

He looked back toward the stairway in the foyer. "I think

it's time we talk to Jack and my grandmother, find out where they got married and what they had to do.''

"You mean you want to get married now? Today? Up here?'' She stared at him.

He nodded.

Epilogue

Gina glanced out the window as they passed Hazel's Café and the motel. Although it was late in the afternoon and snow was falling, there was a vacancy sign. Not too many motorists on their way to the lake would be stopping at Lascott, not like last year when the blizzard hit.

"So that's where you two stayed?" Ella asked from the back seat of the Lexus.

"Room 106," Randall answered and glanced Gina's way. "Two nights in a sagging double bed."

"Tish, tish. How sinful." Ella laughed and snuggled closer to the man by her side. "What do you think, Jack? Did they behave themselves in that bed?"

Jack Longman chuckled. "About as well as we did that night, I'm sure."

"Ah, but we were married," Ella reminded him.

"We got married as soon as we could," Randall said. "Didn't we?"

Gina shook her head, remembering back to the wedding chapel they'd gone to last year. "We did, but I wasn't sure it was legal, not until we had that second ceremony."

Once again, Jack chuckled. "Now, are you saying that you didn't like our choice of ministers?"

"Someone dressed like Elvis Presley makes me wonder," Gina confessed.

"Well, the ceremony in San Jose was beautiful," Ella said. "And I thank you for allowing us to join you at the altar."

"You women just wanted us dressed up in monkey suits," Jack grumbled and leaned forward to tap Randall's shoulder. "Don't you agree?"

Randall looked at Gina and smiled. It had been worth dressing up in a tuxedo and going through the ceremony again to see her in a wedding dress, her eyes sparkling with excitement, her cheeks flushed. And the second ceremony had been more solemn. No scratchy record playing "Love Me Tender," no minister swiveling his hips and chanting "Yeah, yeah" when Gina said, "I do."

Both marriage ceremonies had been legal: the one at the wedding chapel and the one in the church. He'd checked. And now they were celebrating their first anniversary, and he knew his decision to marry Gina had been the smartest move he'd made in his life. Oh yes, love was a gamble. His mother had lost more than once and he would always have Maureen to remind him of the risks, but the gamble was worth it when you hit the jackpot.

Up ahead, cars slowed, then pulled to the side of the road, and Randall saw the reason why. Though the snow wasn't coming down as heavily as it had a year ago, enough had accumulated on the highway to require chains. He had a pair in the trunk. This time he'd been prepared. Instead of chasing after his grandmother, all four of them would be spending a week at Jack's cabin. They would share an anniversary and Gina would continue his ski lessons. It would probably be the last time she would be on skis before the baby was born.

He glanced at her bulging stomach and thought back to the first time they'd made love. He'd thought he could get her out of his system. What a fool he'd been. What a lucky fool.

"Are you going to pull over and put on your chains?" Gina asked, her gaze meeting his.

He considered it, then considered the alternative. Funny, he'd never thought of himself as sentimental, but he was discovering a lot of things about himself that he'd never thought true. He glanced toward the back seat and spoke to Jack and his grandmother. "Would you two mind if we go back to that motel in Lascott and spend tonight there? I can't say the beds are great, but that restaurant next to it serves great chicken and hamburgers."

"You want to go back to Lascott?" Jack asked, disbelief lacing his words. "But we're not that far from my place."

"If they want to go back, we're going back," Ella said firmly. "It's their anniversary as well as ours."

Randall looked at Gina. "What do you say?"

She smiled, then glanced back at Ella and Jack. "You'll love Hazel's Café. It's an experience."

As Randall steered the car around, Gina felt a kick in the ribs from the baby she was carrying. Soon she and Randall would be a family of three. They were both looking forward to the event. The happiness they'd found in each other would only be multiplied, enriching the years to come. Love might be a gamble, but she knew theirs was going to pay off.

* * * * *

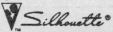

Take 4 bestselling love stories FREE

Plus get a FREE surprise gift!

Special Limited-time Offer

Mail to Silhouette Reader Service™

3010 Walden Avenue
P.O. Box 1867
Buffalo, N.Y. 14269-1867

YES! Please send me 4 free Silhouette Yours Truly™ novels and my free surprise gift. Then send me 4 brand-new novels every other month, which I will receive months before they appear in bookstores. Bill me at the low price of $2.90 each plus 25¢ delivery and applicable sales tax, if any.* That's the complete price and a savings of over 10% off the cover prices—quite a bargain! I understand that accepting the books and gift places me under no obligation ever to buy any books. I can always return a shipment and cancel at any time. Even if I never buy another book from Silhouette, the 4 free books and the surprise gift are mine to keep forever.

201 SEN CF2X

Name	(PLEASE PRINT)	
Address		Apt. No.
City	State	Zip

This offer is limited to one order per household and not valid to present Silhouette Yours Truly™ subscribers. *Terms and prices are subject to change without notice. Sales tax applicable in N.Y.

USYRT-296

PAULA DETMER RIGGS

Continues the twelve-book series— 36 Hours—in May 1998 with Book Eleven

THE PARENT PLAN

Cassidy and Karen Sloane's marriage was on the rocks—and had been since their little girl spent one lonely, stormy night trapped in a cave. And it would take their daughter's wisdom and love to convince the stubborn rancher and the proud doctor that they had better things to do than clash over their careers, because their most important job was being Mom and Dad—and husband and wife.

For Cassidy and Karen and *all* the residents of Grand Springs, Colorado, the storm-induced blackout was just the beginning of 36 Hours that changed *everything!* You won't want to miss a single book.

Available at your favorite retail outlet.

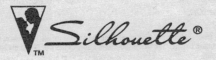

Catch more great
HARLEQUIN™ Movies
featured on the movie channel tmc

Premiering May 9th
The Awakening

starring Cynthia Geary and
David Beecroft, based on the novel by
Patricia Coughlin

Don't miss next month's movie!
Premiering June 13th
Diamond Girl
based on the novel by bestselling author
Diana Palmer

If you are not currently a subscriber to
The Movie Channel, simply call your
local cable or satellite provider for more
details. Call today, and don't miss out
on the romance!

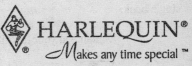

100% pure movies.
100% pure fun.

HARLEQUIN®
Makes any time special ™

Harlequin, Joey Device, Makes any time special and Superromance are trademarks of
Harlequin Enterprises Limited. The Movie Channel is a service mark of Showtime Networks, Inc.,
a Viacom Company.

An Alliance Television Production

HMBPA598

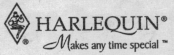

RETURN TO WHITEHORN

Silhouette's beloved **MONTANA MAVERICKS** returns with brand-new stories from your favorite authors! Welcome back to Whitehorn, Montana—a place where rich tales of passion and adventure are unfolding under the Big Sky. The new generation of Mavericks will leave you breathless!

Coming from Silhouette Special Edition®:

February 98: LETTER TO A LONESOME COWBOY by Jackie Merritt

March 98: WIFE MOST WANTED by Joan Elliott Pickart

May 98: A FATHER'S VOW by Myrna Temte

June 98: A HERO'S HOMECOMING by Laurie Paige

And don't miss these two very special additions to the Montana Mavericks saga:

MONTANA MAVERICKS WEDDINGS
by Diana Palmer, Ann Major and Susan Mallery
Short story collection available April 98

WILD WEST WIFE by Susan Mallery
Harlequin Historicals available July 98

Round up these great new stories
at your favorite retail outlet.

Silhouette®   Look us up on-line at: http://www.romance.net

SSEMMF-J

Silhouette Books
is proud to announce the arrival of

A MOTHER'S GIFT

This May, for three women, the perfect Mother's Day gift is mother*hood!* With the help of a lonely child in need of a home and the love of a very special man, these three heroines are about to receive this most precious gift as they surrender their single lives for a future as a family.

Waiting for Mom
by Kathleen Eagle
Nobody's Child
by Emilie Richards
Mother's Day Baby
by Joan Elliott Pickart

Three brand-new, heartwarming stories by three of your favorite authors in one collection—it's the best Mother's Day gift the rest of us could hope for.

Available May 1998 at your favorite retail outlet.